A COLLECTION OF DESIRES

7 TALES OF MODERN HORROR

SHAWN C. BAKER

For Kirsten.

SCARE ME

The film school intelligentsia was out full force, holding court and casting aspersions on the various indie cinema coming attractions posted to the columns of the Egyptian Theatre's outdoor courtyard. In the sky above, the pale moon played duck and cover behind an uncharacteristically dense cloud mass, underlit by the ceaseless pulses of light pollution that bled skyward from the various Hollywood Boulevard happenings. These mostly invite-only functions - screenings, tech company to-do's, and indie flick wrap parties - formed a daunting veneer that wrapped around the theatre like some massive tentacle, slowing squeezing one of the last vestiges of old Hollywood into the entropy at the center of an exclusionary black hole. Apple's relationship with this part of town was a volatile mess at best; she loved the more subtle instances of Hollywood's culture as it infiltrated places that would have otherwise been lost to the attraction and commerce, hated everything else.

Especially the hipsters.

Lucas, on the other hand, looked as happy as she'd ever

seen him. Apple watched him as their flirty banter lulled and afforded him the opportunity to peruse the crowd assembled in the courtyard. He smiled with a sense of satisfaction the likes of which was altogether out of place among their jaded and cynical group of friends. Apple had known Lucas only a short while, but she knew him well enough to know these were the nights he lived for; the people around them were those he viewed as peers. In anyone else, this bristling positivity would have annoyed her to no end, but with Lucas, there was such a sense of wonderment that she found her own cynicism hard-won in its presence. It was probably the thing Apple liked most about him; Lucas made her feel like a better person, if only for a little while.

But of course, she'd never admit to that.

"Looking for someone more interesting to wait in line with?"

"Is it that obvious?"

"Sad clown face," she said and kicked the toe of his converse. They both laughed.

"Sorry. I guess I kinda spaced. That was pretty good weed."

"Yeah. Anyway, I don't know if it's going to get a wide release, but if they're smart, it'll hit Prime or Netflix in a month or two. Great Anthology."

"Awesome," Lucas responded, still distracted and unsure what movie they had even been talking about. He'd caught sight of two guys in matching blood-red polo shirts moving through the queue with glowing tablets, stopping to chat with people seemingly at random. He followed their path through the crowd for several minutes, and the continued conversational abandonment made Apple's endearment turn a little sour around the edges.

"You know, I don't even know why I come out to these

premieres anymore. The fucking audience just ruins the experience."

Her sudden negativity caught Lucas's attention.

"Aw come on, don't be a hater."

"I also hate the word hater."

"That's bullshit, and you know it Apple."

"No it's not; I really hate the word hater."

"You know what I mean, the shit about the crowd. These are fans, just like you and me. It's not like this is the AMC in Del Amo mall. You come to Hollywood for a film premiere; this is what you get."

"Arthouse snobbery? Half of these douches aren't here for the movie; they're here for cred."

"Really? Look at that guy; I mean, that's awesome. Where do you get a t-shirt for a Joe Begos flick?"

"Yeah, okay. That is pretty cool."

The guy in question saw Lucas and Apple looking at him and gave a concerned shrug as if he should recognize them but didn't.

"Your shirt," Apple assured him, "It's awesome."

Pressure off, the guy smiled with the triumph reserved for the fan that wins the other fan's approval.

"Thanks. Made it from a screenshot."

"Killer," Apple smiled and turned back to Lucas.

"See," she said.

"Okay. Sorry. I guess I've been locked up in my place for so long that I'm used to the idea that all horror fans are as fickle as the trolls online."

"Don't mistake the virtual world for the real one. You confuse the two, things get ugly."

"Hey guys, how's it going?" another Redshirt asked approaching from behind them.

"What're you selling?" Apple asked, claws out.

"Whoah. It's totally not like that."

"Really? What's it like then?"

"She means we're really just here for the movie man, not any, um, whatever extras."

"Great! That's why we're out here, for the movie."

"We already have tickets."

"Great! Psyched?"

"He is. I'm here for the ride."

"Really? Not a horror fan?"

"Why would you assume just because I'm not 'psyched' to see this particular movie that I'm not a horror fan?"

"Come on Apple," Lucas admonished tiredly. Apologetically he turned back to Redshirt, "Sorry man. She's a critic; doesn't like anything."

Redshirt laughed and made a conceding gesture with his hands, shifted his stance to focus on Lucas. Apple mouthed 'fuck you' and turned away, their good-natured fun spoiled by the intrusion of a third party.

"Okay, so you're looking forward to the flick?"

"Yeah. Yeah, I guess I am. I mean, sounds different, ya know?"

"Definitely. So, speaking to that, would you be interested in participating in a one-of-a-kind experience designed to enhance the film?"

"Um, I don't know? Sell me."

"Alright!" Redshirt said and moved in closer to show Lucas the images on his tablet. The screen glowed crimson red. "The director wanted to integrate mobile technology in a way that parallels the tech in the film, so he developed an app. It's an interactive game designed to bring the movie to life, so it doesn't have to end when the lights come up."

"Sounds cool. How's it work?"

"Check this out," Redshirt opened an icon on the screen that looked like a cartoon skull. It was the kind of thing that would adorn a pair of kid's tennis shoes or a t-shirt ordered via a Facebook ad, "You download the app and then turn it on right before the movie starts. There are interactive signals that run between the film and the app."

"Wait, how does that work? Exactly?"

"Don't worry. You'll receive the standard permission requests when you first open it. Nothing too intrusive. Scare Me uses your camera and microphone to 'communicate' with the film. Then, when the movie ends, the app creates an environment designed to imitate it utilizing your operating system."

"Isn't the movie about an app that kills people?"

"Ha, no, not really," This guy had Lucas on the line, and he knew it, he didn't have to bother with Apple anymore. But she wasn't about to let him off that easy.

"All the press would seem to indicate that was the plot."

"As a critic, I'm sure you're aware that in the age of viral marketing, movies sometimes employ disinformation campaigns. You know, to avoid spoilers before anyone's even seen them," he turned back to Lucas and the smile resurfaced, "Your friend isn't totally wrong, but, well, think of Scare Me as Fincher's The Game meets Pokemon Go."

"Sold! Fucking sold man - one of my favorite movies from one of my favorite directors."

"Bomb dude. Alright, let me just start with your email address and then..."

Apple rolled her eyes and turned away from them, mouthing the words 'Bomb' and 'Dude' while making the Norman Bates stabbing gesture with her left hand. She scanned the crowd hoping for a bit of non-douchebaggery to offset the nightmare behind her but saw nothing of the sort. Her scan stopped when she saw the other Redshirt. From across the courtyard, he stared at her with a smile that made her skin crawl. She'd seen that smile before; it came from the same impetus that made guest users on her site say things like, "women don't understand horror" or "chicks should only be cast as body parts." Apple had put up with shit like that for a few years before she gained enough notoriety to squash it by requiring an email for log-in. Redshirt seemed to recognize her thoughts; his smile broadened.

Something bumped against her thigh, and Apple flinched as the line around her began to move.

"Hey, c'mon or we'll miss the flick," Lucas said and playfully pushed her by the shoulder.

"Yeah, like we're not going to get a seat with what, like seventy people here."

Lucas looked defeated, "Man, you just can't have any fun at all, can you?"

"Fuck off," Apple said but knew he was right.

The movie was as uninspired as she'd expected and while they filed out past the concession stand, Apple scanned the crowd for either of the Redshirts. She really wanted to tell them what a waste of time they'd chosen to endorse. Neither were anywhere to be found.

"Wow. Hope the app is better than the flick because that kinda blew."

"Oh, so it wasn't, like, bomb dude?"

"Fuck off. But yeah. Ha, Evil Dead it was not," Lucas joked, clearly trying to save face after all the hype he'd regurgitated to her over the weeks since he'd bought the tickets.

"Whatever. I'm sure if the movie that cost twenty million dollars to make left you feeling cheated then the stupid app is sure to save the day," Apple would never in a million years admit it, but the film had actually gotten under her skin. There was something ineffably disturbing about watching a movie about an app that killed people directly after her friend had signed up for a make-believe version of the same app.

"I guess I'm a dumbass, huh?" Lucas said, guard down.

Here he was, the guy Apple would never admit she couldn't get enough of.

"Yeah. Dumb ass," she said and moved out in front of the post-movie throng that clogged the courtyard. A little way up she spotted the door to their favorite watering hole, the Pig and Whistle; Apple was thirsty and not even close to done giving Lucas shit.

She had to force her way through a cloister of long-haired, sexless fanboys to reach the door and when she did, she realized Lucas was no longer behind her. She looked back and saw him stopped in the middle of the courtyard, his eyes trained on a red light emanating from his phone. Irritated and a little creeped out, Apple put two fingers in her mouth and let out a loud whistle. Lucas looked up and his quiet lucidity shattered as he became aware of the twelve or so other people standing around him, all staring into the same glow from their phones, all now looking at Apple.

"You look like a bunch of fucking zombies!" she yelled and disappeared into the cool, dark atmosphere of the Pig.

~

An hour later they each were beginning their third pint of beer. Things had relaxed a bit, despite the fact that Apple continued to dodge her concerns by teasing Lucas for buying into the film's gimmick.

"So can I expect a snotty comment or two when I post my review?"

"I wouldn't necessarily go that far. I mean, the more I think about it, the more I can say I definitely didn't hate it, but go ahead and trash it."

7

"Thank you for your permission Lucas," they laughed and as if on cue the waiter popped his head over the low wall that divided the dining area from the bar seating. He gave an inquisitive nod, to which Apple responded, "Two shots of Bushmills."

The waiter - Gary she thought his name was - spun the index finger of his free hand in as enigmatic an invocation of service as either of them had ever witnessed.

"Is it just me or have you never heard that guy say anything like, ever?"

"Probably trying to break into the silent film market, I hear it's making a comeback."

Apple laughed at Lucas's joke; it re-affirmed something invisible and intimate between them. Her snark subsided; she was willing to hear his thoughts, despite her own opinion.

"Okay, so what is it exactly that you liked about the flick?"

"I keep going back to that scene in the theatre. There was such a sense of something bigger. Something... cosmic."

The scene in question had been of a particularly disturbing nature to Apple. It dealt with a large number of people trapped inside a theatre much like the one they had been in, images on the screen coming to life and butchering them one by one.

"You're just saying that because of how meta the whole thing was."

"You think?"

"Ah, hello? You downloaded an app with the same name as the movie right before it started. If that's not meta, I don't know what is."

"But Meta is so dead. This was... I don't know. What's the word I want?"

"Pretentious?"

"No... well, yeah. Maybe," Lucas stood and retrieved his phone from his pocket just as the shots arrived.

"Be right back, gotta hit the head."

"You take too long, and I'm doing your shot," Apple only half-joked as Lucas walked toward the hall in the back of the bar with his face once again buried in the eerie red light.

When he returned, Lucas frowned at the sight of the empty shot glass in front of him. He signaled the waiter for another round and then killed the remainder of his pint in two large gulps.

"Trynna to catch up?" Apple asked, one hundred percent aware she had officially begun to slur her words. Lucas didn't respond at first, didn't even make eye contact with her. She noticed his phone no longer commanded his attention. He appeared frazzled. Lucas's brother had been sick lately; she hoped he hadn't received bad news.

"Hey, what's up?"

"It works," he said without raising his head.

"What?"

He looked at her, visibly shaken.

"It works. The App."

"What happened?"

Lucas looked around for a moment, then continued, "You know the hallway to the stairs?"

"Yeah."

"Well, something weird just happened in it."

To get to the restrooms in the Pig and Whistle, you walked through a long hallway mirrored on both sides. At the end of this corridor was a room for private parties to the right of which were two small flights of stairs set at ninety-degree angles to one another. These led to the lower floor and the restrooms. Also on that floor was the entrance to a weekend nightclub the venue hosted. Neon tubing above the club's door read "Sinners."

"I got a text from Sam but, well, I'm not so sure it was actually from her."

"Sam as in Samantha?" Samantha was another local in the scene, a girl who went by the handle "gravebayby" on social media and wrote for a horror news site called deathbycelluloid.com

"Yeah, it said she was downstairs in the club."

"Let me get this straight. You didn't really have to take a leak at all; you were ditching me for Sam?"

"I was gonna invite her up to sit with us. Oh, come on Apple. Shit, I figured if she was here it probably meant she was at the screening too. Figured you could both gang up on me. You know Sam would hate it as much as you. More maybe."

"There's a lot to hate," Apple paused to take a drink. She hadn't realized Lucas and Sam knew each other as well as it now appeared they did.

"So what'd she say?"

"That's just it. At first, it looked like a regular message, but then I realized it came in through the app."

"You mean, like, the app is using your contacts?"

"Masquerading as them is more like it."

"Okay, that's fucked up. Delete that shit like now."

"I know, I know, but look, it's... I don't know. There's something about it..."

Lucas held out his phone so Apple could see the screen; a scrolling table of images underlit by the now infamous red light caught her eye, beckoned her to look closer. She held it to her eyes, and immediately the room changed under the influence of the app: the table across from them had skeletons seated around it and a severed head in the center. A dead raven crucified on a makeshift cross adorned the wall above the door. At the bar, an androgynous corpse hung upside down by veins stretched from its arms. The images were all ghoulish in theme but cartoonish in portrayal, perfect matches for the skull logo. Apple scanned the room, and out of the back corner a very realistic bat with a human child's face flew by her, buzzed so close that Apple flinched, almost fell out of her seat.

"Whoah! That was fucking crazy! It looked real."

"Yeah. So I was looking through that when I headed into the hallway. Through the phone's camera, my reflections got all corpse-like. Rotting. I stopped to try and figure out how it worked, and that's when I realized there was someone behind me. It was a big guy with a skull mask that looked just like the logo. But he wasn't there when I looked without the phone, so I figured neat trick, right?. Then I swear to god Apple, someone touched me on the shoulder. I jumped like ten feet in the fucking air."

"Dude, that's crazy," Apple said, only half listening to him. The view through the phone had her complete attention. The images darkened in tone and the room became a slaughter-house. Bodies littered the aisles, stacks of flesh torn into little more than scraps of bloody pink paper. It mirrored a scene from the second act, the movie's reality superimposed over their own.

"This is fucked."

She was about to hand the phone back to Lucas when Gary the waiter walked by carrying a tray of empty glasses toward the mirrored corridor. As he did, Apple noticed a series of red X's on the back of his neck; freshly cut and styl-ized wounds that dripped with fleshy chunks of blood.

"Jesus," she said and lowered the phone to try and assess the scene without it. No dice, the waiter had already disap-peared into the mirrored hallway.

"Apple, are you even listening?"

"I'll be right back," she said and darted up and after the waiter.

The bar had become considerably more crowded, and as she dodged bodies, Apple lost sight of her quarry. She hit the hallway with the phone still in front of her eyes. At once Apple saw what Lucas had been talking about: through the lens of the camera, the walls and floor disappeared, leaving only a black space that throbbed with the movement of hundreds of her reflections. She tried to follow one of them, but focus only caused the image to degrade. The effect made her feel nauseous, as if she was somehow witnessing a time lapse of her life. Beneath these apparitions, Apple sensed something else. Something sick and withered.

She pulled the phone away from her eyes just in time to see the waiter disappear down the stairs that led to the bottom floor. She followed, passing the backstage room and noting a dull bass throb that emanated from behind its guard.

Apple took the first eight stairs, turned the corner and started down the next eight. Below and to her left Gary, the waiter disappeared through the door marked Sinners, the pink neon light pulsing with enough juice to illuminate the bloody Xs on the back of his neck.

Apple stopped halfway down the second flight of stairs. The phone was still in her hand but she realized she'd lost track of whether or not she'd been looking through it the whole time. Reality buckled under the pressures of the digital interface and disorientation folded in around her like great black wings. Alarmed, Apple misstepped on the next stair, stumbled for a moment and only caught herself on the wall just before tumbling the rest of the way to the floor below. She stood there for several minutes, holding her awareness on the phone in her hand, concentrating on the difference between its version of reality and the real one. At the bottom of the stairs, the club door slipped open a crack and the neon light popped once and went dark. Apple traversed the remaining stairs slowly, reaching for the door-knob but stopping when the door opened the rest of the way on its own and a human figure emerged from the darkness beyond its threshold.

"Sam?"

It was Samantha, the girl Lucas had come down to meet. All but a few errant strands of the flesh on her face had been peeled away, hanging around her jaw like the skin of a moist, red banana. The muscles that coated her skull peeled her mouth back in something lost between a grin and a grimace. Samantha stopped a few feet from Apple and reached out in what looked like agony before finally crumpling to the floor like a pile of clothes that had, for the briefest of moments, learned to pretend they were human. Apple only recognized Sam by her trademark long, pink pigtails.

Apple screamed. Behind her strong hands secured her shoulders and she turned, her left fist connecting with the firm texture of flesh and bone. Something inside two of her knuckles popped and the phone clattered to the floor. Before her Gary, the waiter cried out in pain and backed away toward the men's room.

"Dude, what the hell is wrong with you?"

They stood face to face, breathing heavy, the waiter's question hanging in the air. On the ground, before them, all signs of Samantha's apparition had disappeared. Terrified and more than a little embarrassed Apple responded to the question the only way she could think.

"I think I've had too much to drink."

~

"Lucas, this thing is dangerous. Delete it."

Lucas did not respond. They had finished their drinks at the Pig and begun the walk home. Despite his experience and resulting concern, Lucas's fascination with the app appeared to have returned; after her own experience, Apple was not about to let it go.

"Hell-Ohwa? Delete the fucking app. Why are we even still talking about this?"

"Apple, it's just a game."

"Yeah, well, it's made by a deranged third party - an unknown third party might I add - that now has access to your entire life. You checked your bank account lately?"

This stopped Lucas cold. Standing where they were on the quiet residential street of Fountain Avenue, bathed in the soft peripheral radius of light cast by a nearby street lamp, Lucas pulled his phone from his pocket and plunked in a couple of numbers. The moment expanded with tension while they waited for the banking app to open.

"You sure you're not giving it access to your account right now? Just by entering your password with that thing on your phone?"

"It's not an AI Apple, Jeez. Okay, there, see? Everything's in order. False alarm. Now can we just drop it?"

They walked a few steps and stopped when the shrill metal cacophony of garbage cans crashing to the ground came from an alley a little ways up and to their right.

"What the fuck was that?"

"Lucas, this is Hollywood. Who cares? Probably a couple of homeless guys fucking."

There was another small clattering of metal on metal, and then a high-pitched female scream shattered the night. Without hesitation, Lucas took off running toward the alley.

"Hello? What the fuck are you doing?" Apple yelled as she

followed him, stopping at the mouth of the alley. The world around her crackled with the raw energies of calamity and danger.

"Lucas!" She screamed. No answer. She took a step into the alley. A hundred feet or so ahead a streetlight flickered briefly and came back weaker.

Several minutes went by. The scream did not recur, nor did any other sound for that matter. Just when she thought she'd reached the end of her ability to cope, Lucas re-emerged.

"Well?"

"Nothing."

"What do you mean nothing?"

"I mean no one was there. I found this though," he held up a piece of paper.

"You going through people's garbage now?"

"Shut up and read it," Lucas handed her the paper. Its texture was filthy and moist; just touching it made Apple's skin crawl. She turned it over and read:

Love Scare Me?

Scare Me Too: Doorways to Blood

Thursday, 9/16

Free Screening

"Part two? Jee-zuz! The first one just premiered. I find it astonishing that the people who made that piece of shit we just watched could possibly be ambitious enough to have made two movies at the same time. I mean, who does that besides like, Robert Zemeckis? And the title? Doorways to Blood?"

"It gets better. C'mere."

"Into the creepy alley? Nope, drawing a line."

Lucas took Apple by the hand and pulled her, "You don't

get to say no."

"You sound like a football player I knew in high school."

"Haha. Seriously, I need you to tell me if I'm losing my mind."

"Let me save us both some time: You're batshit dude," Apple said but allowed Lucas to pull her into the alley and along the snaking curve of the two high wooden fences that gave the route its shape.

"Here."

The fence on the left had a small alcove with two plastic garbage cans in front of it, the street light Apple had noted before directly above them. Behind these was a door set into the fence, and Apple was overtaken by a feeling of unreality as she realized its surface was nearly completely covered with a dripping, viscous crimson liquid.

"Is that blood?"

"Can't be real. But yeah, that's definitely the effect they were going for."

"Who? The effect *who* was going for Lucas?"

They stood staring at the door for a few moments before Apple realized it was partially open.

"Jesus Christ. Lucas, it's open!"

"What? He took a step forward and Apple yanked him back so hard by the arm that he almost lost his footing on some loose gravel.

"Let's get out of here, okay? I'm drunk, I'm tired and I was hoping you'd invite me in for a nightcap."

Lucas's eye flared like candles caught in a draft. A tiny smile crept into his face.

"A nightcap, huh?"

~

Sometime after the clock in Lucas's living room struck two Apple slipped from bed, grabbed the laptop from her backpack and headed to the kitchen. She started the computer and went to the fridge to snatch a bottle of IPA. She drank deep, her body thirsty for the beverage. When she felt slightly quenched, Apple took a seat at the small Formica table and began to work. Sleep had provided inspiration and she had a few random thoughts on Scare Me she wanted to get out before they sluiced through the drain and disappeared forever. Hours after the bizarre events that had concluded their evening Apple still found herself considerably more upset than she wished to admit. The only way to combat this was to write a review of the film and tear it to pieces.

When she finished the review, she posted it to her site and then downed the rest of her beer. As she stood to get another, she noticed the folded piece of dirty paper on the table. She plucked it free from the small puddle of condensation left by her bottle and reread, the feeling that she'd somehow missed the point resurfacing and making her feel slightly frustrated:

Love Scare Me?
Scare Me Too: Doorways to Blood
Thursday, 9/16
Free Screening

Inspiration struck as she opened the new bottle. Returning to her computer, Apple googled "Doorways to Blood." A moment later she was lost down a rabbit hole of links, flitting from blogs to articles to tweets. It took her a few minutes, but eventually, Apple found what she was looking for: a review of a Peruvian film named Puertas a la

Sangre that had premiered earlier in the year. The piece, written a little over six months ago, belonged to none other than gravebayby, aka Samantha.

The image of Samantha's fleshless face resurfaced and Apple hammered it with two long pulls on her beer before beginning to re-read the article she'd originally glossed over upon its initial publication.

In her review - which was scathing - Samantha discussed seeing the film at a festival in Buenos Aires last March. It was what she called a "terrifyingly exploitive 90 minutes of trash". Sam went on to say that there had apparently been some kind of conspiracy surrounding the film, as rumors that several people had actually been murdered during the filming of a key sequence in which a ritual sacrifice took place had reached the Argentinian government and caused a shutdown of subsequent viewings. Turned out Sam had been present for the only screening of Puertas to date and she very much regretted having happened into that honor.

Reading the piece again, Apple's head began to spin. There was something so forlorn about Sam's regret at having experienced the film that Apple found herself in an uncharacteristic spiral of empathy. Usually, she adhered to a strict ethos of taking responsibility for one's own actions, however, the idea that Sam had gone in to see a horror movie and ended up witnessing something that had, in Sam's own words, "fundamentally changed her, and not for the better" infinitely saddened Apple. She'd only met Samantha twice, both last year at horror-related cons, but she liked her. They'd quickly developed a kinship as two of the only females writing in a mostly male-dominated niche. It was a small comfort in the macrocosm of Apple's daily anxieties but it was a comfort nonetheless.

After a while her reverie ebbed and, devoid of any significant amount of exhaustion by which to return to bed, Apple grabbed another beer from the fridge. It was the last so she made a mental note that no matter what she would have to run out and buy Lucas more tomorrow before he returned from work. Her buzz from earlier now re-ignited, Apple finished reading the article and then googled Scare Me Too, the idea that the sequel might be a remake of such a nefarious film as Puertas a la Sangre seeming inevitable but incongruous. Scare Me was three rungs down the ladder from standard studio horror fare, a modern version of The Ring, while Puertas was exploitation; raw and mean and not meant for mass consumption.

A small Ping startled her and Apple realized Lucas's phone was sitting on the counter behind her. She spotted it and couldn't help feeling her own internal ping; who was texting him at three in the morning?

She knew she shouldn't but she'd had more than enough alcohol to motivate a bad decision. She finished her third beer of the session and walked to the fridge to get another, remembered there were none left and deftly segued into picking up Lucas's phone instead. The screen was never locked so the moment she ran her finger across its surface the device lit up with the now infamous crimson glow she'd learned to associate with the app. Apple watched as the opening graphic dissolved in an effect that mirrored blood running down the screen. Behind it was the flashing cartoon skull. Its oscillation suggested participation and in spite of herself Apple double-tapped it.

A video file opened and began to play. It was dark; a moving shot along what appeared to be a residential street at night. Two people walked a path in front of the camera that-

Apple dropped the phone.

It was them. It was Lucas and her earlier that evening, walking back to his place from the bar.

〜

When Apple woke up, it was dark outside. At first, she thought she'd only been out for a moment; disoriented she sat up and everything came back to her. She climbed from the bed expecting to find Lucas in the kitchen. Instead, she found a note taped to the refrigerator.

Left you some coffee and there are toaster strudels in the
freezer. Apple, last night was awesome but...
You drank all my beer!
-Lucas

Apple rubbed the sleep from her eyes and tried to gather her wits. Whatever she'd been dreaming still clung to the inside of her skull with vague, amorphous talons; it was hollow and weakening and stirred vestigial feelings of sickness and death inside her. Why was Lucas's note so easy going? Why hadn't he woken her up? The idea that he'd not seen the video yet at, what? What time was it?

The clock on the microwave said 7:30 PM.

"Seven-thirty? Holy shit."

She poured some coffee into a black ceramic mug that had, "All work and no play make Lucas a dull boy," printed all over it in blood red letters. In her mind, she replayed the image of their trek home from the Pig as captured by an unknown third party and the feeling of revulsion, of total violation slipped back over her like a black bag tied firmly around her head. It stifled her, made her cringe in horrible anticipation.

Apple grabbed her phone, began to text Lucas. She had wanted to wake him when the video had come through but the problem of explaining how she had seen it, of why she was going through his phone was definitely one she wanted

20

to avoid this early on in whatever it was that was developing between them.

She looked at what she had begun to text, deleted it to start again. She still had to be careful about how she worded her concern.

Apple: Hey you. How's your day? I slept allll the way through until just now. TY 4 the coffee BTW. How's your stupid app?

Apple hit send and waited. It was ridiculous, she knew, waiting for an instantaneous response. She looked at the time on the phone. The microwave was off by an hour. Still, 7:30 and she was pretty sure Lucas should already be on his way home from work, which if she remembered correctly was just down the street on Hollywood Boulevard.

She poured more coffee and laughed at the idea of the strudels. Her stomach was knotted; she wouldn't be eating anytime soon. Even the coffee felt like acid as it went down. What Apple really wanted was a beer.

She hesitated at the impetus, then set the mug in the sink and went to the fridge.

"Does it really count as drinking for breakfast if you wake up at 7:30 PM? Don't think so."

The moment before she opened the refrigerator door Apple remembered drinking the final beer the night before.

"Shit!" she went to the window - a light but consistent rain was falling, "Looks like someone's getting wet," she said, pulling on a hoodie she found on a nearby chair.

Her phone buzzed with a notification. It was Lucas. At the same moment, Apple stopped to read his text the sound of footsteps came to her from just the other side of the door.

Lucas: If anyone comes to the door DO NOT ANSWER

Apple's nerves froze as she turned her attention to the door. Her ears strained. Had she imagined the footsteps? What about Lucas's text?

A loud, dull knock shattered her ability to explain the situation away rationally. Afraid, Apple approached the door.

"Hello?"

Nothing. Then, soft, tittering laughter.

"Fuck this."

The phone buzzed again.

Lucas: I'll be home in ten minutes. DON'T GO OUTSIDE NMW

Ice coated her spine as Apple stormed back into the kitchen and removed a large, serrated knife from the sink, its surface still stained with the brown, dried remains of whatever Lucas had used it for last. Blade in hand she took a deep breath, puffed herself up and marched back to the door, throwing it open with the knife ramrod straight out in front of her.

Nothing.

"Jesus Apple, relax."

But she couldn't; ahead of her on the sidewalk she saw a hunched, dark figure heading toward the street.

Pulling up the hood Apple stepped out into the rain and ran the cracked sidewalk path; Lucas rented a guest house and as she maneuvered past the main house Apple lost sight of the figure. When she passed through the gate, she did so just in time to see Lucas come splashing around the corner down the street. He stopped short when he saw Apple with the knife and she realized he didn't recognize her with the hood up.

"It's me! Lucas, it's me!"

Re-assured, Lucas began to run again and when he reached Apple grabbed her free hand and led her back down the path toward the guest house.

"Dude, what are you doing outside?"

"Someone was knocking on the door."

"Didn't you get my text?"

"Yeah, but..."

A loud peal of thunder cut her off as they arrived at the door and recoiled at the sight of another flyer stuck to it.

Free Screening!
Thursday Night
Scare Me Too: Doorways to Blood

"Oh my god," Lucas said, staring at Apple with tears in his eyes.

~

"You're going to have to slow down Lucas; I'm not following you at all."

Lucas sat back in his chair and took a long pull off the bottle of tequila Apple had found in the back of his cabinet. His face convulsed as he drank and Apple remembered Lucas previously saying he hated tequila; the bottle must have been left by someone else. If she remembered correctly, Sam liked Tequila...

"Any port in a storm," she said under her breath.

Lucas finished his draw and set the bottle back down, pushing it as far away from him as he could reach across the table.

"Did you get a look at them?"

"No. Now back to you. What happened? What made you text me that?"

"I... something terrible happened," he said, a pall falling over his features.

"Enough mystery. Tell me."

"Were you on social media today?"

"A little bit."

"Did you hear about Sam?"

23

Chills.

"No. What happened?"

"She's dead."

Two words that had all the subtly of an explosion; the room seemed to fill up with smoke and mortar as choking black clouds of shattered potential and lacerated memories threatened to topple the remainder of Apple's sanity.

In her back pocket, Apple's phone began to buzz.

"What happened?" she asked, terrified enough to want to throw her phone in the garbage disposal.

"I don't know exactly. I went to Death by Celluloid to kill some time and Garrett had a big article memorializing her. It said she'd been found by a friend late last night, which he only knew because he had by trying to reach her for an article that was due and a fucking cop answered her phone."

"Did Garrett say what article?"

"Yeah. Sam was beta testing the Scare Me app."

"I told you! Goddamnit Lucas," Apple's chair skidded back against the chalky white tile of the kitchen.

"Yeah. You told me alright. And I didn't listen and now... now someone's dead."

"Okay, start at the beginning, will you?"

"I... I got pretty fucked up when I heard. I was going to message you but... I don't know; something just blocked that, you know? Like I needed to be alone with it for a little while. So I clocked out early and went to Powerhouse for a beer."

"By yourself? Dude, I knew her too."

"Yeah but, I knew her more. We... Apple, Sam and I hooked up after last year's Horror Hound Weekend."

"So?" she said doing a bad job pretending the revelation didn't bother her.

"It didn't have anything to do with her messaging me the other night, if that even was her. Sam and I, we were... I don't know. We were just a thing, okay? As you may have noticed I dig horror chicks, so what can I say? The opportunity presented itself and I couldn't pass it up at the time."

"She's not a fucking job opening you pig."

"You know what I mean. Don't play all virginal with me."

Apple backed off. She was betraying her cool, detached persona.

"So it happened a few times and then, well, I think she met someone else. I don't know. But we still talked here and there. Just friends, you know?"

"I get it."

"Okay, so when I got to the bar, I started playing with my phone and that stupid app started going off. I had messages, messages that mentioned Sam. That told me things about what happened to her."

"Tell me you're kidding."

"Wish I could. It didn't use her name, but it was like, like a Tarot reading, all very indirect. It said 'YOU could have saved her.'

"Jesus."

"You're telling me. So I sat there and drank and tried to figure out the app. You know, like I went into the preferences and googled the manufacturer. Everything and anything I could think of. You know what I found?"

"Let me guess: Nothing."

"Exactly. So there's me, after two hours, hammered and freaked out. I mean, I'd worked myself into a fucking state. Eventually, I had to piss but it was like as soon as I became lucid I realized the bar was packed. I didn't want to have to deal with those small ass bathrooms and all the weird shit that happens in them on nights with a crowd, so I pounded what was left in my pint and left, went into that alley around the side of it."

"The one with the Chaplin mural?"

"Yeah. But as I walked deep enough into it to piss, I realized someone was hovering around the entrance. I really had to go, so I didn't let that stop me, but then while I had my junk in my hand my phone started buzzing. So there's this escalating moment of anxiety as I'm pissing against the wall and the phone's buzzing - I mean, it just would not stop - and I realize the person at the end of the alley has started walking towards me."

"Oh shit."

"Yeah. I get this fucked up feeling and fish my phone out of my pocket and there's the red glow. I look at it and there's a message blinking on the screen in black letters. It takes me a second, cuz I'm drunk and my attention is already split three ways, and I realize just as the shadow of the person approaching is almost on top of me what it says."

"What'd it say?"

"'Apple won't answer the door.' And it's punctuated with that little cartoon skull. I turn and it's the guy from the hallway in the Pig and Whistle, the one I saw while looking through the app."

"The one with the skull mask."

"Yeah. I totally freaked out. Ran out of the alley, ended up on some street I didn't recognize. And the guy, the shadow or whatever, he was still behind me."

Apple's face slackened with horror.

"Jesus fuck."

"Yeah. That's pretty much what I said too. And the whole time the fucking phone just keeps buzzing. Not like one continuous call but a series of notices or updates or whatever. I dogged up McCadden and then back up Yucca to Highland, a block from Powerhouse, where the intersection with Franklin is. The light had just changed to Don't Walk and man, Apple, I just darted right out across traffic. It was like I couldn't get past the idea that the guy was tracking me through the phone. So I went for it, and just like you'd expect, there's horns blaring at me and an SUV almost hit me. I don't know what they were doing but I mean, like, they just missed me, swerved at the last minute and... Apple, they t-boned the driver's side of a Taurus in the other lane. I mean, it was fucking bad, man. Real bad."

Lucas was in tears again.

"Lucas..."

He held up his hand to silence her, gathered his strength to continue.

"I just stood there staring, in the middle of the street. In the middle of fucking Highland. And all these cars were blaring their horns and people were getting out screaming at me and then... some guy grabbed my arm... I mean, I don't know if it was the guy that was following me or if it was just some passerby, but I turned and hit him as hard as I could in the face. And then I ran."

Apple stood and began to pace. Lucas took another hit from the bottle and returned it to the table. Apple picked it up and quaffed enthusiastically. Somewhere in her head, she'd rounded a corner. If this had happened to Lucas, then she wasn't going insane. That meant everything to her because it allowed Apple to begin to formulate a plan.

"How many people do you think those Redshirts signed up that night?"

"How the hell should I know?"

"I saw you watching them. They weren't approaching everyone in the crowd, were they?"

"Didn't look like it, no."

Apple thought for a moment. Lucas reached out for the tequila; she handed it to him. He hit it again pretty hard, looked like he was about to puke.

"We have to go to this premiere."

"Apple, are you fucking nuts?"

"Lucas, we can get a shit ton of people together. Think

27

about it - they only approached a small group of people. They're not equipped to do this to more than a few people at a time."

He was silent because he knew she was right.

"What time did you send me that message about not opening the door?"

"It was right when I ran out the back of the Chaplin alley.

"Okay, so it seems like the time frame between the message you got and the knock at the door is off, so they're not well orchestrated. That suggests limitations."

"Maybe, but what if that's just the 'street team.' Don't forget whoever designed the app."

"Plus the Redshirts. Unless whoever's doing this is just piggybacking off the app somehow. Like someone with a backdoor in, that can access what Scare Me pulls from people's phones."

"How the hell do we prove that? How do we prove any of this?"

"We don't. Lucas, let me make some calls."

The premiere was at 9:00 PM, so Lucas showed up early and took a sidewalk table at the little hipster cafe across La Brea. This was about 6:00 PM. To relax his nerves, he ordered a pint of dark beer and waited. He wore a ball cap, dark clothes, and sunglasses. Sitting at the little, wrought-iron table, sipping the beer on a 70 degree California evening, Lucas began to worry that his attempt at being inconspicuous might have had the opposite effect. After a while, he realized it didn't matter. If whoever was doing this to them really could track him by his phone, they would never know he was there; he and Apple had switched phones earlier in the day, so they'd be following her instead.

Lucas had felt funny letting Apple take the crosshairs, but in the end, her plan was the best chance they had. The only chance. And frankly, Apple seemed to be dealing with the entire scenario considerably better than he was so he figured she could take care of herself.

At about 7:00 PM, Lucas watched two nondescript workers in white overalls put up the title of the movie on the faded marquee in front of the theatre. Apple had made a pretty convincing argument as to why she was certain Scare Me Too: Doorways to Blood was a remake of Puertas a la Sangre, a movie Lucas remembered vividly talking to Samantha about after she'd seen it. Back in March, the two of them were still somewhat involved. When Samantha arrived home from the Buenos Aires film festival, she'd shown up at his place at two in the morning with the bottle of tequila and a need to divest herself of what she called, "residue of the sickest shit she'd ever seen." She had related how she'd met the director of Puertas before the film, had shaken his hand, and then conducted a confrontational Q and A with him after the viewing. According to her Garrett at Death By Celluloid had wanted to post the interview but changed his mind at the last minute, a decision that ran one hundred percent contrary to his editorial style. Sam had wondered at the time if Garrett had received threats and Lucas had told her she was being paranoid.

"She sure showed me."

He hadn't seen Sam since that night, had, in fact, become worried about her mental state after talking to her on Messenger several times and seeing that whatever the movie had done to her had not abated but had appeared to have increased in its effect. None of this was anything he felt he needed to share with Apple; it didn't change their situation, just exacerbated it.

The sun went down and the marquee lit up; the theatre

itself was old and dingy, but still notable as a Hollywood landmark. He'd been in it once, several years back, and remembered feeling a bit claustrophobic at the time. The queue for entry would form on the sidewalk, as inside there was only a lobby and the one theatre, so when their group entered altogether their presence, depending on how many people Apple could roust, should make an immediate impact. As long as she was functioning; Lucas had noted Apple's encroaching alcoholism shortly after starting to hang out with her, and he hoped she wouldn't be finding her courage for tonight's plan by starting early.

But then again, who was he to say anything?

Lucas finished his third pint and waved to the waiter for one more.

"Last one," he said as he handed off his empty.

Flashbacks to the traffic incident on Highland assailed him as he bolted across La Brea and caught up with Apple and her friends, two of whom he knew, two of whom he did not.

"This is it?" he asked, acknowledging Garrett, a cosplayer that went by MissPain (real name Misty), and the two people he didn't know as the line stopped just before the ticket taker at the door to the theatre.

Apple nodded, and Lucas could tell by the way she moved her head that she had at least a few in her already.

"Last minute. Plus, well, most of my outreach was ignored."

"Yeah, the older people get, the more they try to ignore their friends when they suffer mental breakdowns. At my age, it's like looking in a mirror on a bad day."

Lucas laughed awkwardly at Garrett's joke and waved

hello to the others. Miss Pain was the only one who looked like she had any idea of what she was getting herself into; dressed in a blood-splattered nurse's outfit she carried with her an oddly carved walking stick and a can of gasoline. Battle prep disguised as cosplay?

"I assume that's empty?" he said, smiling.

"Let's hope they do too," she responded with a distinctly unsettling smile.

Apple reached the door first. An older woman with an unenthusiastic smile ushered them inside.

"Enjoy the show."

"Excuse me, but do you know if the filmmaker is here this evening?"

The woman, five-three, and easily no more than one hundred pounds, looked as though she was in her late fifties. Her poorly dyed red hair, generous application of makeup and non-existent breasts gave her a distinctly androgynous look.

"I'm sure he's around here somewhere. Bunch'a 'em came in earlier, set up the marquee and everything. Real DIY."

They passed through the door and Lucas pulled Apple aside.

"She's lying. I watched two guys in overalls set everything up."

"Then she's in on it," Apple responded without slowing down. She led the six of them back past the concessions - which was stocked but not open - and through a partition in the red velvet curtain. Behind this was a double door through which they emerged into a theatre already popu-lated to just over half its capacity. The sight of the crowd stopped them short.

"What the hell?" one of the other two unknowns Apple had brought said a little too loudly. Several of the folks sitting in the back rows turned to look at them with deep, needy eyes.

"They just opened the doors, where did all these people come from?"

"Let's find out," Apple said and took several confident steps forward. She raised her hands to garner the room's attention.

"Hello, everybody! My name's Apple and I'm here with some friends representing Death By Celluloid magazine. How's everyone doing tonight?"

Everyone in the house not already looking at them turned in unison. It was creepy, and Lucas thought lent the scene a certain 'Stepford' vibe. The silence buzzed like malevolent electricity as an entire room full of people stared at them but no one volunteered a word.

"Is everyone looking forward to the movie? I know we are, right guys?"

The same unknown friend answered with a hesitant 'yes' and then immediately crumpled his shoulders as he realized Apple hadn't been appealing to him. It was the room she was trying to engage with, and the room's only interaction continued as silent, awkward staring.

Miss Pain shivered.

"Talkative group, eh?"

Just as Apple looked to be floundering for something more to say, the lights went down and the screen became a bright, pulsing red. The cartoon skull they had learned to associate with the app flashed on the screen.

"Jesus, talk about unceremonious."

In the confusion to find a seat, a figure made its way up the aisle toward them. It was a girl, and as she brushed past Lucas the lights flashed, and he was certain for a second that it was Samantha. He turned to get a better look, but the girl had already passed through the curtain and out into the lobby.

"What the... Apple? Garrett? Did you see that? I think that was Samantha."

"What?" Garrett asked as the skull image dissolved into a door of blood and a series of high pitched screams began to pummel their ears through the sound system.

"Apple!" Lucas screamed, but Apple was already moving deeper down the aisle. He didn't want to leave the group but a strange feeling had come over him. The girl who passed him had her hair pulled into two tight ponytails, exactly the way Sam always did.

He had to know.

"I'll be right back," Lucas said, his voice drowned out by more screams as the door on the screen began to open. The last image from the film Lucas took with him as he passed back through the red curtains and out into the lobby was a violent, limned shadow crossing the threshold of the door, stepping out of the...

"No," he said to himself, suddenly terribly shaken by the image. In his head, it had actually looked as though the image was crossing the threshold of the screen, not just the door on the screen.

"Impossible."

"What's that honey?" the ticket taker asked, now seated on a gold and crimson-upholstered bench, smoking a filterless cigarette.

"I, uh..." it was hard for Lucas to remember why he'd left the theatre in the first place, something about Samantha...

"Sorry. I'm not feeling all that great."

The woman patted the upholstery beside her and Lucas sat.

"Who're you looking for, sweetheart?"

"A... a friend I guess. I thought I saw her walk out of the theatre a minute ago."

"Well, I been sitting here for quite a while and I didn't see anyone leave. Was it the pretty one with the big mouth you walked in with?"

"No. Different one. I guess, um..." Lucas stood, suddenly embarrassed, "I'm sorry. I think I drank too much or something," he turned to re-enter the theatre.

"Sorry deary, the movie's already begun. No re-entry."

The ticket woman's words hit Lucas like a bucket of water.

"What do you mean no re-entry?"

Exhaling what looked like a lethal amount of smoke, the woman nodded her head at a sign posted above the red curtains:

No Re-Entry Once Movie Has Begun

"Fuck that."

Lucas turned and went back through the curtains only to find the double doors locked. From inside the theatre, he heard more screams and a low-end rumble that sounded like a motor.

"Them's the brakes kiddo."

"What the fuck is going on? Open the goddamn door!"

"No can do. Orders from the big guy."

Lucas turned back to the door and tried again. The screams were louder now and sounded like they were coming from the people in the theatre rather than the movie screen. A loud thumping started, and someone began pounding on the other side of the door.

"Hey, I think something's happening. I think the people in there need help!"

"Ya ask me, anyone who comes to see shit like this needs

help. Not my battle kiddo," the woman said with a curt smile. She stamped her cigarette out and stood, started for the door to the street.

"Hey! Where you going? I need your help!"

"Not me kid, I got another gig in half an hour. Sorry 'bout your friends."

The woman exited through the door and vanished around the corner. Lucas was left alone in the lobby of the theatre, the sound of the screams coming from behind the door rising to a fever pitch. In his pocket, his phone buzzed and he quickly furrowed it from his jeans and opened a new message. It was from Apple. Or it wasn't. The red light of the Scare Me app glowed in his hands and he remembered that this wasn't his phone, it was Apple's. The message read:

"Thank you for signing up for Scare Me! It is our mission to entertain you with a realistic as hell horror-themed environment. Please press 'Accept' to begin your game!"

Lucas pressed accept.

THE APARTMENT

Thursday, December 15th

He watched her disappear down the hall and into the back bedroom, his heart in her hands, blood staining the floor below the fist in which she carried it.

Tuesday, December 13th

Firelight lit the inside of the bar with the hazy glow of memories, many of them good, but most of them bad. Kraig's had been their bar; a place of celebration, contemplation and, when appropriate, mourning.

"So what brings you back here after all this time?"

Devlin had expected dirty looks and indirect fuck you's upon his hometown return, but he had not expected them from Cole. He and Cole had been tight.

"Just needed time to hole up and get some money saved. Shit's tough right now in LaLa Land. Rent is killing me."

Cole smirked a little and Devlin felt the desire to turn around and walk back out the door. Instead, he persisted.

There was too much history between the two of them to throw away on bullshit. And besides, Dev knew he'd left Cole in the lurch when he took off five years ago, so he was ready, willing and able to take his fair share of abuse. The operative word being 'fair.'

"Seriously man, I just wanted to look you up, say hey and shoot the shit. Figured I owed you an apology for leaving the band high and dry. If you're not into it, you know, no harm no foul."

"Fuck off."

"Fair enough. See you around, Cole."

Dev almost made it to the door before Cole stopped him.

"Get back here dickhead."

Cole stood. Dev walked back, and they embraced in the big, exaggerated way men over thirty on the South Side of Chicago embrace: self-conscious from the ever-present background radiation of homophobic paranoia. Dev remembered this; he remembered what it was like to live here, beholden to suspicion and prejudice. As if on cue, their hug ended with the big, open-handed pats on the back that Dev would have bet on, an ostentatious assurance to everyone in the bar that these two men didn't need to 'get a room.' They were just dear, recently reunited friends.

Now that everyone more or less knew where everyone else stood, they sat down and Cole signaled the bartender.

"Christie, give this son of a bitch whatever he wants, on me."

The bartender, a rode-hard-and-put-away-wet blonde in her early 60's, flashed her eyes at Dev.

"Makers and water," he responded.

Christie disappeared around the side of the bar, and Cole put an arm around Dev and pinched his shoulder with all five fingers.

"Man, I always knew I'd see you again someday, just doubted it'd be anything like this."

"What did you expect?" Dev said and accepted the tumbler of whiskey from Christie.

"Honestly? I thought I'd see you somewhere wearing some big, 'I'm the shit' grin. L.A. and all, ya know?"

"You really think that's me?"

Cole thought for a moment, sipped his beer, a pale glass of German lager that looked lukewarm at best.

"Naw, guess not. I don't know though Dev, didn't think it was you to walk away from our music either."

"We were going nowhere shackled to those two morons. I mean, seriously, was the result what you wanted?"

"We never made it that far."

Devlin sipped his drink; he had nothing to say to that.

"You're right though; we weren't there, but we weren't really headed there anymore anyway. I knew it; I was just afraid of another ending. You know how long it took me to find anyone to play with after Murder Dolls? I couldn't do that shit again, writing fucking songs in my apartment, wasting time. Shit, we're fucking thirty. Thirty. With half the shit you n' me done, I ain't expecting to live too much past fifty, and I sure ain't expecting to enjoy a lot of those last ten years, so I got what? Ten years left at best?"

"We were twenty-five at the time. We could have started over."

"Yeah well, I did."

Dev paused with the glass on his lip, disturbed by the idea that his friend and one-time collaborator had actually moved on.

"Didn't expect that, did ya?" Cole asked. He pounded the remainder of his pint and stood.

"I got next," Devlin said.

"Fuck you."

"Nope. Fuck you, Cole. I got next. If we're gonna trade stories and play catch up, we're going round by round."

Cole laughed, slapped Dev on the back as he headed toward the men's room at the other end of the bar.

"No dickhead, I meant fuck you, I want an upgrade if you're buying. Get me Jameson on the rocks."

"Same old Cole."

The night progressed in a slippery fashion. Devlin sensed a somewhat frightening imbalance in Cole; something was troubling him, had been for a long time. He listened to Cole talk about his new band with a growing sense of jealous despondency because maybe Cole hadn't needed Devlin at all. Things sounded good; better than Devlin wanted to know, a situation that sounded light years ahead of the dysfunctional douchebaggery that had hounded them at every turn in Rituals. That band had been fine when it was just a side project, but once Cole's main band the Murder Dolls imploded, Cole had made Rituals his primary focus and brought in a rhythm section, two guys he knew from the remains of the local scene. Unholy Ritual became a full-on live act, and things turned sour fast.

For starters, Jimmy and Gordon - drummer and bassist respectively - hadn't been in a coherent group for years. Both were older than Dev and Cole by about ten years, both had waxing and waning junk habits, and both had definite ideas about where Cole's eerie good looks and Reznor-esque vocals could get them. The thing was, they didn't think the musical material fit the same aesthetic. Or at least, that was the argument on the surface. In reality, Devlin had always harbored the suspicion that Jimmy and Gordon were afraid of the Occult subtext to the music he and Cole wrote. Either way, Ritual hadn't been designed as a democracy, and neither Dev or Cole were going to accept two aging ne're de wells suddenly having input into their material.

"See, with this new shit, it's safe. I'm done with the Magick because, well, frankly Dev, I ain't so sure we 'closed the loop' on that last one."

Dev's spine prickled. The idea that they had left something undone was something he'd not even considered.

"What'd ya mean you aren't sure? We did everything we were supposed to."

Cole sat back and smiled that weird, leathery smile he had. You could see two decades of bong smoke in those creases around his mouth when he was happy, which admittedly was seldom.

"Yeah, but I don't trust that we didn't fuck it up. Hallucinogens and Magick do not mix. You remember I told you that at the time?"

Devlin was silent. The event Cole was referring to centered around a song they'd written. It was an unsettling piece; a make-shift aural voodoo doll meant to conjure one of a series of Demonic Intelligences and use it to bolster their success. Devlin and Cole had spent forty-eight hours writing and recording this thing of intricate beauty, performed and recorded it in Cole's living room and then Jimmy and Gordon had refused to play it, refused to even listen to it all the way through. Gordon had said something about 'bad vibes' and Devlin had almost throttled him straight away. Not even a month later, Dev had packed up and moved to Los Angeles, soon as he could save enough to ensure he'd hit town with first and last month's rent. It had all gone a lot easier than he'd anticipated and as a result, Devlin had always read that as validation for his actions.

"Water under the bridge. Ancient history man. What aren't you telling me, Cole?"

"Ancient history to you maybe, not to those of us who've had to live here for the last five years."

"It's not like we didn't stay in touch online."

"Please."

"Well, if it was so bad why didn't you call me?"

"What would I say? Besides, I didn't catch-up of this right away. Then, what? I just call and say, 'hey Dev, put down your Kale salad and fly home, we left a demon in my old apartment."

Both men paused to finish their drinks and Devlin jumped up and signaled Christie, whose speed at filling their glasses had already made her his new favorite bartender. Something told him he was going to need another before they continued.

Beverages revived, the two men settled into the heart of the matter before them.

"Okay Mr. Enigma, talk."

Cole laughed.

"That banishing ritual we used? Incom-fucking-plete brother. We left that thing there man. Left it to feed on other people."

Cole had titled the piece The Eyes of Pahadron, Pahadron being the Angel of Terror in ancient Hebrew mysticism and all its various, not-so-nice offshoots. Like the other pieces they wrote occult programming into, Pahadron was a ritual intended to be performed as a song. This gave their new bandmates the creeps. It'd given Devlin the creeps too, but back then, that feeling was what he thrived on. The night he and Cole recorded it they did so under the influence of hallucinogens, solitude, completely focused on the obscure minutiae that both expected would give the piece a chance to actually work. In terms of the occult, both Dev and Cole were used to implied results, not the kind of holy-shit-that-worked

41

outcome they read about in books by Crowley, Mathers, and Wincott. Pahadron was different. Pahadron had been designed to work.

"What do you mean incomplete? We wrote that thing out, line for line, note for note. We couldn't have missed anything."

"I'm not saying we missed it in the planning stages. But in the moment? Well, do you remember any of it? 'Cuz I certainly don't. That's the problem: we fucked up."

Devlin's interest in the Occult could be traced back to his early adolescence. A loner, Devlin had fallen hard into the new wave of British Comic book writers; guys like Alan Moore and Grant Morrison; students of the Occult that incorporated the practice into their art and then talked openly and enthusiastically about it. Hell, Morrison had practically given his avid readers lessons when he began publishing his 'Pop Magick' articles around the turn of the century. Dev had jumped in head first.

"How?"

Cole drank deep and leveled his eyes on his friend.

"Six months after you left I moved out of that dump. A couple of months after that I heard from one of my cop buddies that a tenant was murdered in that building. When I asked him the apartment number, bam. 203."

Devlin's spine turned to ice, and without even realizing it he drained his glass. Reality flickered. There was probably a rational explanation. The thing was, a substantial part of him didn't want this to be rational in any way. This was it, what they had always wanted. Something, anything, no matter the cost. He closed his eyes and squeezed the bridge of his nose and the word SUCCESS appeared in the darkness, about thirty feet high and spitting flames.

When Dev opened his eyes again, Cole was staring at him. Smiling.

"Yeah, that's right. It worked. Just not how or when we planned."

"I don't understand. How did you continue to live there and nothing happened to you, then as soon as you move out this started?"

Cole reached into his shirt and loosed the necklace that hung there, a silver Pentacle.

"Started wearing it about the time we wrote Pahadron. Bought one for you too actually, only you had your little tantrum before I had the chance to give it to you."

"Jesus."

"Yeah. I ain't fucking wit choo bro. We summoned something and then left it in that apartment."

Devlin realized his glass was empty again. What's more, he was starting to slur his words. A full-on drunk was on the horizon, and he had no intention of removing his foot from the gas pedal anytime soon, not with news like this.

"Anyone live there now?"

"No. Wanna know why?"

"Why?"

"Because the next person that lived there died, too."

"Jesus!" Devlin shouted, and the entire bar turned to look at them.

"Fuck off," he said to the room, even as Cole made a conciliatory gesture with his hands.

"Cool out, or we'll be looking for another bar."

"Fuck man. How the fuck did this happen? Why?"

"Hey. Hey!" Cole's hand shot out and clamped Devlin's left arm.

"We can take care of this, okay? Just keep your fucking cool, brother. It's you and me again, just like the old days."

Christie approached, and Devlin held out his glass without looking at her.

"You can have water. You drink that and keep the

outbursts to a minimum, and I'll consider giving you a beer. No more whiskey. For either of you."

"Goddamnit..."

"Easy Dev. He's fine Christie. We both are. And you are, as always, correct. Two waters and two Kostritzer's."

Christie hesitated for a moment and then returned to the bar, brought out two tall glasses of water.

"Call me when you finish these, okay sweetheart?"

Cole smiled at her, then returned his gaze to Devlin.

"What'd your cop buddy tell you about the second death?"

"I didn't find out about the second one from Dave. The second one was Jen."

Devlin's jaw nearly hit the table. Jen was Cole's ex-wife; she and Devlin had dated for about a year after high school and, truth told, he'd never gotten over her. Then, in their early twenties, she and Cole had gotten together. Devlin tried not to let it bother him, and mostly it didn't, but when he thought about it - which wasn't often - he usually recognized that their union had created a kind of resentment mask he wore around Cole, despite their closeness. A year later - two before Dev left for LA - when Cole told him he and Jen were getting a divorce, Dev breathed a sigh of relief. Of course, they'd spoken about all this at the time, shared a few beers and ruminated on the tall blonde whose voice could melt your heart right before she stabbed you in the back.

"What the hell was Jen doing living there?"

Cole smiled. To Devlin, it sounded like he was enjoying telling the story.

"We started talking again about a year ago. Jen's mom got sick, and she called to let me know. Ended up on the phone for a long time, buried the hatchet. So six months ago she happened to mention she was looking for a place to live in the area, but her credit's fucked. I told her I knew the landlord."

"Jesus Christ Cole! You pulled strings to get Jen into a place you thought this thing... this thing..." Dev didn't have the apparatus to describe what they were talking about; it was too big, too vague and ineffable.

Cole smiled.

Devlin's brain reeled with his attempts to balance the person he thought he knew with the person before him. They were not the same.

"That's so fucked. I mean, FUCKED with a capital fucking F Cole."

Devlin stood.

"What? That too much for ya? You leaving?"

"I'm going to piss."

~

"You're a fucking psycho; you know that Cole?"

Cole smiled, set a fresh drink in front of Devlin. Beer, but it'd have to do.

"So you believe me now?"

Dev hesitated for a moment. He was staring it in the face, this belief. He'd heard that Jen had died, hadn't heard how and hadn't particularly cared at the time. Now he felt like as big an asshole as Cole. And if what Cole said was true, then it was just as much Dev's fault as his.

"I don't know if I believe you. Let's just say I don't *not* believe you for now, okay? Where does that leave us?"

"Well, I thought once you heard, you might want to help me go back and take care of it. Clean up our mess."

"Meaning what, exactly?"

"We gather the proper materials, break into the apartment and get rid of whatever it is we left there. So no one else has to die."

Devlin couldn't believe what he was hearing, couldn't understand how it made sense, but it did.

"I take it no one is living there at the moment?"

"Whole fucking building's abandoned."

"What about the landlord?"

"Don't know. I had Dave check on it for me - looks like the guy disappeared; building's in limbo while some relatives fight over it."

"So we can probably assume he's a victim too."

"Guy was a dick."

"Jesus, Cole."

"Jesus ain't gonna help us old buddy. You want to try'n clean up your conscience; this is the only way to do it."

"What makes you think my conscience is going to bother me?"

Cole surprised Devlin by pushing his chair back from the table and standing up.

"Tell you what. You think it over, let me know if you have trouble sleeping next couple nights."

The smug grin still firmly entrenched in the flesh of his face, Cole finished his beer in two gulps, turned and walked through the large oak door that had the word "KRAIG'S" etched into its knotted surface. On his way out the door, without turning around Devlin heard him say, "Sweet dreams, bro."

The first thing Devlin did when he arrived back at the temporary accommodations his parents had made for him was fire up the internet and google Jen for information on her untimely demise. According to the plethora of local news articles about her death, Jennifer Osterberg had died in her apartment on 95th; cause of death was blunt force trauma to the back of the head. No weapon found and, disturbingly enough, no evidence of forced entry at the scene of the crime either. Police had no leads. That was six months ago.

After finding no mention of the other death in the apartment, Dev surfed back to about the time Cole said he had moved out. That building held most of his good memories with Cole: late nights getting stoned and working on music, watching horror flicks and, increasingly near the end, researching and rehearsing occult rituals. Devlin had done a lot of similar stuff with his Uncle Martin when he was in high school - drawing large-scale pentagrams and peppering them with the names of Enochian Dukes and Magistrates, supposed angels that the literature of the Art said could be accessible for guidance and, sometimes favors. And where Cole had traipsed right into these Magicks with reckless abandon, Devlin's caution had mostly curbed what sometimes felt like dangerous sessions. Martin had warned Devlin about contacting these beings; he had been of the opinion that these kinds of entities were actually manifestations of deeper parts of the practitioner's own psyche. Martin used to warn him that when dealing with these things you had to be certain of the kind of people you were involved with; an unbalanced psyche could taint the working and create a toxic event. Cole had always been a great friend to Dev, but his moral compass skewed considerably left of center.

They wrote Pahadron's Eye on a Thursday night, performed and recorded the piece right there in Cole's apartment and one month later Devlin was on his way out of Chicago, the band a bad taste on the back of his tongue.

Until now; that bad taste climbed back up out of Dev's stomach as he located several articles on the first death in the apartment. It was similar to Jen's insofar as the method, but differed in one important respect. The victim, a middle-aged sous chef who worked at a local restaurant, had complained several times to the police that someone was breaking into his apartment at night and watching him sleep.

～

Wednesday, December 14th

Lunch with his parents, followed by dinner and a movie with his sister and her husband, and Dev's mind had adequate stimuli to prevent it from wandering back to the grim circumstances that tainted his return. By midnight though, he was alone and found himself unable to think of anything else. Ill-advised perhaps, Devlin borrowed the keys to his Dad's pick-up truck and drove out to Cole's former apartment. Sitting in the parking lot at two in the morning, Devlin couldn't help feeling as though there was something Cole had missed in the ramifications of their situation. As he stared up at the balcony, Devlin thought he could see a light through the newspaper that covered the sliding glass door. He stared for a long time, imagining Jen and how she had died, if she had suffered, if who or whatever had killed her had watched her the way they had Cole's successor.

Around four Devlin circled the lot on his way out and noticed with no small amount of intrigue that the entrance on the south side of the building was ajar.

～

Thursday, December 15th

"Thought I'd see you again sooner than later."

"Yeah, well you forget Cole, my uncle taught me a lot about this kind of thing."

"I know he did," Cole said. He took a drag from his cigarette and ushered Dev into his small studio apartment with unceremonious triumph. Cole always liked to be right, and it didn't help that he usually was. Devlin walked in and hovered awkwardly in the small area between the front door and the rest of the pad: a king-sized bed against the far wall, a small couch closer to him and an old-school television that faced it. On either side of the set were bookcases, every shelf of which contained either horror movies or books on the occult. To his right, the blinds were half-drawn on a sliding glass porch door with a view of 115th Street. The door was partially open, and Dev looked out on a crisp night, traffic moderate for a Friday evening this close to Christmas and only three blocks from the mall. Something dark and viscous streaked the glass in several places.

Behind him, Cole shut the door. It was full dark outside, and as Dev would have bet, Cole had only candles for light. He moved past Devlin and plopped onto the couch, stubbed his cigarette out in an ashtray that Devlin knew read "All work and no play make Cole a dull boy" in crimson red letters. Jen had given it to Cole their first Christmas together.

Slightly uncomfortable, Devlin avoided sitting next to his old friend by moving to the bookcases. Scanning the spines, Devlin noticed two books that were his, that he had lent Cole back during the band days: Crowley's Illustrated Goetia and Mather's translation of the Grimoire of Armadel.

"Couple of those are yours."

"Keep 'em."

"Don't practice anymore?"

"Not so much." Not at all was more like it, but Dev refused to give Cole information he thought would make him feel any more superior than he already did.

"How come?"

"No time," Devlin answered without turning around.

49

Daily life had pushed his interest in Magick to the outskirts of his Universe, and being here with Cole, under these circumstances, made that seem like the best decision he'd ever made.

The candles flickered in the draft from the porch and music crept up from speakers placed strategically around the room. He recognized it the second he heard it:

Pahadron's Eye.

Devlin turned and held Cole's intrusive gaze.

"You trying' ta be funny?"

Cole smiled.

"Oh come on."

This was the problem with Cole, the one that drove so many people away. Reality had to be whatever he said it was.

"When was the last time you listened to anything we did?"

"Ages," Devlin lied. He listened to several of their albums regularly. Just not this one.

"I listen to our stuff constantly."

Cole produced half a joint from the darkness and lit it. Without thinking Devlin moved in and took it as Cole exhaled. He drew a big hit, held it in and waited for the silver stars to bubble up in front of his eyes. When they came, they were stronger than he'd expected.

"Holy shit," he said hacking up smoke. Devlin's balance teetered, and he dropped onto the couch and bent forward, put his head between his knees until he could breathe properly again.

"Quit smoking too?"

"Yeah, a while ago."

"Well, I'm honored."

Dev looked up and smiled, "When in Rome, you know? Okay, so Cole, what do we do?"

Cole hit the joint again, and when Devlin refused it, he

carefully stubbed it out in the ashtray and lit another cigarette.

"Well, we figure out what we're dealing with, gather the appropriate articles and go in and banish that fucker back to where it came from."

"Man, if Martin were here he'd say we were fucking crazy."

"Martin ain't here."

"Yeah, well if he were I'd be going to him for help."

"Well, unless you want me to pull out my old Ouija board so you can attempt to contact him, I guess we're on our own."

"Would help if we knew what we were dealing with."

Cole stood and crossed to the bookcase, removed a dusty tome with a tattered black dust jacket and opened it to a marked page in the last third.

"Well, there were three major names I set out to evoke with this one. Pahadron, Belial, and Lucifer."

"I think we can safely assume you didn't manifest the big guy and leave him stranded on the South Side," Devlin said, wondering what a demon anthropomorphized from Cole's subconscious might look like.

"Didn't Martin ever teach you that in Magick there is no such thing as 'we can safely assume'?

Cole had him. Devlin's internal psychoanalysis machine kicked in, and he realized that he had come into this ready to downplay everything, not because Devlin didn't believe it was really happening, but because he didn't want to have to deal with it. Devlin looked again at that ashtray and knew they had to deal with it.

"So where do we start?"

"We start at the end. At the place. I get off work tomorrow about 11:00 PM. Meet me here about 11:15 and I'll drive us over."

~

Instead of heading home when Devlin left Cole's he took a little detour and cruised by the apartment again. This time he entered the parking lot the way he had exited the night before, and sure enough, the door was still ajar.

~

Friday, December 16th

The drive up Cicero started out quiet save for a local rock station Cole kept low in the background. Zeppelin's Kashmir droned just below the sound of the tires on the road, and Devlin realized he'd not heard this song in years. It made him feel distant from himself, from the person he once was. Then he realized that detachment was exactly what he'd wanted to feel when he'd moved. Considered now, he was unsure if this was good or bad.

"'What's your take then?" Cole asked, nodding at the book he'd given Devlin the night before. Dev had forgotten it was in his hands, his fingers worrying its dilapidated cover. It was handmade and poorly so, its spine a jagged series of uneven knots, the loose fabric of the cover torn and infected with topographical pockets of dust. There was no name on it, only the faint outline of an obtuse geometrical shape on the reverse.

"Well, looking over the pages you marked, I've got to assume we're dealing with Pahadron."

"Why?"

"Because he doesn't have anything better to do. Seriously, there's next to nothing online about him except one standard refrain on only a handful of pages," Devlin dug in his right front shirt pocket and withdrew a piece of paper; unfolding it he read:

"Pahadron: Regarded in Jewish Mysticism as the chief angel of Terror. Rules from September to October."

"Nothing better to do? You watch the fucking news? Terror's big business, it wins elections, makes the world go round. Terror's everywhere, and where there's terror, there's Pahadron."

This was something Dev hadn't considered, the idea that the Hebrew Angel of Terror might be actively loose in their world, shaping it. Was it possible they had let him in? No, that was ridiculous. But they may have tipped some unknown scale in his favor.

Zeppelin gave way to Tool's Undertow, and Cole turned the volume up.

It was a creepy feeling, being this close to something he'd caused and not even known it. Some primordial voice in Dev's brain began to howl, but he held it at bay as Cole made the turn from Cicero to 95th. Was it his imagination, or were the street lights flickering as they passed beneath each one?

Undertow ended abruptly in a burst of static and Cole brought the volume down to a low crackle as they pulled into the small parking lot to the north of the building.

"Okay, I'll be back out for you in a minute."

Cole left the car running when he got out, the radio still barely audible. His secretive demeanor was doing nothing to curb the howling in Devlin's head, and after a few minutes he grew self-conscious at the sound of the engine and reached for the key, cutting the engine but leaving the battery on for the radio. Without the engine, the static resumed prominence and after a few minutes of contemplating the nothingness, Devlin began to think he heard something therein: a deep, crunchy voice just below the lower frequency crush of white noise. He paused before adjusting the volume, trained his ear deep into the oceanic static.

"Return... Another meal..."

A noise outside startled him. From the other side of the window, Cole laughed.

"Get the keys and let's go, we're in."

~

"Definitely empty," Cole observed as they entered.

"Yeah," Devlin responded. There was a dry, rasping echo that crawled atop every step. It made him think of a mortuary. Or maybe more appropriately, a tomb.

"Second floor."

"No shit? How many times I been here, Cole?"

"Just checking, in case you forgot."

A minute later they were at Cole's old door, 203.

"You bring a key?" Devlin smirked.

"Yep," Cole said as he reared back on his left leg and used his right to kick the door in. The barrier didn't come away from the lock, but the center of it splintered enough that Cole was able to tear another board out and reach in to undo the deadbolt. Once unlatched, the door swung away into the foul darkness beyond and a second later they were both standing in old familiar territory.

"Jesus. Did they leave the fucking corpse here?" Cole said, pinching his nose. The room smelled like someone had pissed on a burning pile of garbage, a stench so invasive Dev imagined it as tendrils probing his nostrils.

"Probably part of the manifestation."

"You'd know that if you'd actually read more than the first paragraphs of those pages you marked for me. No wonder this happened. Were you this fucking sloppy five years ago?"

Cole didn't respond.

Devlin breathed in the familiar gloom and saw for the first time a bucket of paint and some tools off in one corner, as if the landlord had been doing some repairs just before he disappeared. Cole passed them on his way down the hall toward the bedrooms. Devlin watched him duck in and out of each room before sliding into the bathroom adjacent to the smaller bedroom. A second later Cole's voice crossed over the sound of his urine hitting the water in the toilet.

"Man, don't come in here. This must be where it happened - there's a massive brown stain on the tub, looks like dried blood."

So Jen had died in the bathroom. Picturing it, Devlin thought about her long, tanned face and there in front of him, down the corridor just outside the bathroom, he saw her. Naked, she walked by the bathroom door as Cole continued to piss, oblivious; she approached Devlin with a smile. On her way, she stopped to pick up a hammer from among the tools.

"I don't know..." Cole said as he came out of the John, still zipping up his jeans, "Sounds like as good a place as any for her to have exited this world, what with all the shit she talked. What?"

Cole's question caught him off guard and Devlin realized he was staring, a blank expression on his face.

"Huh? Nothing, just... just thinking about it; about Jen dying that way."

The howl was louder than ever now, and Devlin realized with no surprise that the hammer was missing.

"Yeah, well, no one else needs to die after-" Cole was interrupted by a loud shriek from somewhere in the building below them.

"Jesus. What the fuck wa s that?"

"I thought this place was empty?"

"So did I."

Devlin had to admit to himself; it was nice to see Cole's bulletproof facade finally crumble. Beneath his flesh, in the nerves and muscles that wrapped around Devlin's insides, an electrical current of absolute terror struck like lightning. His knees and stomach went weak for a moment. From out of the corner of his eye, he could see someone near him, a black shape smiling a huge, toothy grin.

"I'll go take a look," Cole said with unconvincing bravado. He walked back through the door to the hall, apparently expecting Dev to follow. And he almost did, but then there was Jen, naked, a ball peen hammer in her left hand.

"You must have known, even back then, that I had a mean streak in me. Remember your dog? Did you really think a car did that?"

Devlin didn't say anything; the memory was a wound, ripped open and salted without mercy. Somewhere below him, the shriek recurred.

Jen raised a hand and Devlin took one step toward her.

"You came because you're addicted to terror. The entire world is addicted to terror. That is how we have re-made things; in our own image." She brought the hammer up and stroked his chin with the claw side of it, the metal cold and wet against his flesh.

The sound of Cole's footsteps as he approached in the hall outside prefaced his entrance by only a handful of seconds.

"Dude, there's something in here with u-"

Devlin turned on Cole quickly, bringing the hammer up in a tight arc that connected with his chin and took the bones away in a great, sweeping explosion of blood and pulp. When the bottom half of Cole's face fell to the floor, it took several of his upper teeth and half of his tongue with it. The shock was enough that Cole died instantaneously, wide-eyed and for the briefest of moments, terrified. Devlin turned back to Jen and saw her hands between her legs, a look of ecstasy on her face. Behind her, a dark shape shook with delight and made feeding sounds.

"Another meal...mmmm... delicious." She undulated in

pleasure for a moment and to Dev's eyes her visage flickered out, a single frame in the reel, a black-skinned monster too outside the realm of anything he'd ever seen before to even begin to assign values to.

"You must not take their lives so quickly. You will learn." Jen was back. There were some cracks in the facade now, but those eyes still burned with the lust Devlin remembered from their brief time together, little more than kids in a transitory romance but one he could now see he had never fully gotten over.

He moved to embrace her and hardly reacted at all when her hand slid between his ribs and returned the thing she had taken from him.

<<<<>>>>

IN HIS ARMS, SHE FELT LOVED

The sensation was that of being punched in the chest. No, scratch that; it didn't even amount to that much. It was a quick, short thud that reverberated through his body but was quickly absorbed and cast back out as his fist met her face. One. Two. Three. Blood arced through the air between them; little bits of it landed on his chin and left cheek. He didn't want to hit her again, but he knew he might have to. Then he realized the blood wasn't from her face at all, and she had not simply punched him in the chest. Addison looked down the front of his t-shirt and saw the black blade sticking out from just above the middle of his left breast. Blood pumped past the hilt, coated the handle, hit Vicki square in the jaw as she stood before him laughing, one eye black, nose mangled from his blows.

She'd done it after all. She'd fucking killed him.

Vicki stared at the body for a long time. Just like that and he was out of her life for good; problem solved. Slumped across the divide that separated the dining room from the sad, puke-green carpet that demarcated the start of the den, she spent over an hour willing away the ghost of her former husband; the sunlight crept backward across Addison's corpse, ashamed to lend its light to her deed. Fuck it. Addison deserved to die. What's more, he deserved what he got: a violent death.

When the light had left the world, and the cold began to seep in through the cracks in the floor, she roused. Her face still hurt; the blood from her nose had dried over the sides of her mouth, forming something of a sealant that cracked when she finally stood up and went to the kitchen for a drink. Her left eye throbbed, made her not want to look in a mirror anytime soon. A few days in dark glasses was a small price to pay for an accomplishment of this magnitude. It's funny, she mused, how the entropy of an abusive relationship could take control of your hopes and dreams, whittle them down to the microscopic necessity of life and death. And that's exactly how it felt; any compunctions she'd initially had about killing Addison had gone out the window weeks ago; ever since all she had been waiting for was the right moment.

That moment had almost come two days earlier, but then a dark remorse appeared to settle over Addison. They'd spent the day tooth and nail, but by evening things had calmed. Vicki had taken a knife from the kitchen and placed it beneath her pillow while she pretended to read, her thoughts a jumbled mess of fear and conspiracy. The knock on the bedroom door had surprised her; at this point in their lives, it was rare for Addison to leave his nest in the basement, especially after so prolonged a conflict. But the door opened, and there he was, his shadow a withered husk as he crossed the room and sat at the foot of the bed.

There were tears in his eyes.

Tentative, Vicki conceded her attention, one hand on the blade beneath the pillow. The moment reared and died; he addressed her in a terrified voice, raspy sobs choking his words. Addison told her that he was sorry, that if something were to happen to him, it would serve him right. He wanted her to know his behavior stemmed from an event he could not control; not an excuse he specified, but he wanted Vicki to know the truth. More than that, however, he wouldn't say, just that he had not been himself in a very long time.

Then he'd gone back into the basement and not come out again until earlier this evening. The apologist was gone, replaced instead by the demon who, over the past seven months, had consumed the man she'd met and fallen in love with not so terribly long ago. The fight began about money but soon turned into the existential filleting of their lives, what he had done to hers and how she had poisoned his. Frustration bred confrontation and confrontation forced her hand. Punches were thrown. The world turned red and then the next thing Vicki knew she'd buried the knife in his chest. Of course, Addison battered her in response, more in self-defense than sadistic vitriol, but her pain was easily transcended by the incomparable feeling of the blade as it sliced into the meat of her husband's chest. It felt like cutting into an onion with a thousand dollar chef's knife. The word was gratifying. Unbelievably gratifying.

So now here she was, free but not out of the woods yet. The monster was dead, but there was still the body to contend with. She'd not thought this part through, had lack-adaisically planned to imitate a favorite television show and fill a plastic tub with Hydrochloric acid. Faced with it now though, that seemed ghoulish, as if it would somehow be worse than the actual act of taking his life. What she really wanted was to burn him. It was practical, sanitary and historical. But where...

As if on cue, Vicki heard the furnace in the basement kick on.

~

Another hour passed during which Vicki experienced a gnawing sense of inertia. She tried to pretend that the reality of disposing of Addison's body didn't in some way represent a colossal failure on her part, but she could not. She'd always had a thing for 'the wrong guy,' a messy disposition her mother had reprimanded her for since her high school dating years. Interesting then that she'd met and married Addison within two months of her mother's funeral, a rash act Vicki now saw as a final, defiant 'Fuck you' to her matron's admonishments. In hindsight, she understood that her marriage had been a coffin to bury the part of her that longed for closure; a sad attempt to banish the yawning maw of mortality, suddenly opened wide before her in the advent of her mother's passing.

Pouring a glass of water from the tap, as Vicki drank some of the dried blood around her mouth loosened enough for her to spit it into the sink. A chill ran the length of her spine, and she turned, suddenly afraid Addison was alive, watching her.

He was not.

The night after her mother's funeral, Vicki met Addison at a bar. Tattooed head to toe and hot in a throwback grunge sort of way, Addison pushed all her buttons. He brewed his own beer and wrote fucked up fiction, several of which had appeared in some of the horror magazines she read on occasion. Vicki remembered one of his stories straight away. *A Dark and Timely Agent* was published in HellBound late the year before; it had stayed with her because of the terrifying premise: while taking hallucinogens in the woods a teenage boy taps into a primordial aspect of his brain and kills his friends in gruesome fashion. It was very Altered States meets Friday the 13th, two of Vicki's favorite movies. Addison had been flattered she knew it, insisted on buying her a drink. One turned into five. They drank and talked until the bar closed and then wound up in the back of his truck. After their physical union, Addison had driven them to a nearby forest preserve where they commandeered one of the decaying gazebos that housed birthdays and family reunions during the day and strange drug rites after dark. Alone, they lay under the stars and talked for hours, and from that point on Vicki was irrevocably in love.

Around the time their relationship had picked up the inertia that came with six solid months, Vicki's grandmother passed away and left her a small chunk of money. Vicki had been month to month on her current lease for the better part of a year, and in the spirit of their relationship's momentum, she decided to buy a small house and ask Addison to move in with her. He agreed vehemently, and despite the tiny, nagging concerns about his inability to hold down a steady job - he'd been through three since they'd been together - Vicki went with it because she'd never felt so loved as she did in Addison's arms. Those first few months were the best time of her life.

They spent Sundays together, all day and all night. Vicki worked the other six days, and Addison did a part-time gig at a coffeehouse as many evenings a week as he could while hunkering down during the day to work on a novel. This was The One he told her; this would put him on the map. He had ties to someone at Hellbound that had seen the first five chapters and guaranteed they could find him a publisher when it was complete. He just had to finish it.

He set up an office in the unfinished basement of the new house, and it was there Addison slaved away on not only the book but brewing a little something besides his beer. Turns out her man had a degree in chemistry and was extremely versatile at making his own hallucinogenic compounds. This was research, he assured her when she expressed concern - hallucinogenic exploration was where he'd first had the idea for *A Dark and Timely Agent*, which the new book was something of a sequel to. Hesitant, Vicky didn't argue. Drugs had never done it for her, but who was she to impose that on him? Besides, she figured Addison was safer making his own than buying off the street.

After one year, stagnation began to settle over them and with it, anger. Sundays went by the wayside; so did Addison's job. Even a low monthly mortgage can be back breaking on one small income, and soon Vicki found herself in need of a second job to keep the lights on. Several months later resentment set in and their relationship, once so fertile, began to resemble something more in the way of a minefield: Vicki felt Addison's use of hallucinogens had altered the fundamental character of his person. For his part, Addison said Vicki had buried him in a domestic tomb and thus, killed his creative energy. Fights, both verbal and eventually physical became a regular event, and Addison spent more and more time in the basement. By this time, however, she was glad of it; the more she interacted with him, the more she saw the effects of the drug in his mannerisms. Was he ever sober anymore? Was the book even close to finished, or had it simply become a perpetual excuse for him to hate her? Or was there something darker that had set in?

In the weeks just before their final fight, Addison's behavior had become increasingly strange. Because of her long hours, Vicki began to go weeks without seeing him; meanwhile, Addison stalked the house in the middle of the night like a ghost, sometimes moaning, talking to himself. Once, she'd opened the bedroom door to find him scurrying down the hall on all fours.

Vicki talked to Addison's brother, Kearn, but he didn't seem concerned. "Addy's always been weird" is all Kearn would say, as if she should just go with the flow. Vicki would find no help there; Addison's kin were aggressively loyal; if there were a problem, Vicki would be expected to acclimate. And that was exactly what she had done, wasting almost a year of her life in a terrible situation. Eventually, she began to feel his eyes on her while she slept and became concerned for her safety. Had he lost his mind? Was he dangerous? What were the hallucinogens doing to his brain? His conscience? Then, one day several weeks ago, she'd found the mutilated corpse of a stray dog in their yard and knew with a sickening certainty it was Addison who had done it.

From that point on Vicki feared for her life.

If she'd had someone to talk to they'd have told her to go to the police. In hindsight, she wasn't sure why she hadn't. Didn't matter anymore. She had taken matters into her own hands and solved her problem.

Well, *almost* solved her problem. She thought of the furnace again and found she longed for a drink. She took one of the last bottles of Addison's most recent batch of beer from the refrigerator and popped the top off with the corner of the countertop. Taking a huge gulp, Vicki almost choked when something solid caught in the back of her throat. Gagging, she ran to the sink and spat the liquid out; a second later realization dawned on her. She raised the bottle to the light and saw the sediment Addison had taught her often accompanies beer brewed with wheat. Relief set in, and Vicki was able to dispel the dark interpretations her mind had conjured. She took another sip and found the brew was quite good once you got past its slightly offsetting texture.

"Good job, honey," she said, and kicked the corpse in the top of the skull on her way back to the fridge to get another. There were three bottles left, and Vicki figured if she drank them all she'd be just about fortified enough to drag the body into the cellar and fold it into the furnace.

She hoped.

In fact, it only took another beer and a half before Vicki rose to her task. At the East end of the kitchen, directly next to the back door was the entrance to the basement. A single bulb adorned the ceiling just above the stairs, its pull-string easily within reach. The illumination, however, did not extend very far, and standing at the top of the stairs she felt uneasy seeing the darkness that concealed the majority of the subterranean space. In the distance, the furnace clicked on again, and as it did, she saw the briefest sliver of orange light. She knew Addison's office would be just to its left. She'd tackle that next; first, though she had a body to get rid of.

Dragging Addison to the top of the stairs, Vicki considered her options for all of two seconds before a burst of anger swelled up inside her. Motivated by a sudden suffocating hatred, Vicki pushed Addison's legs up over his head and sent his corpse tumbling down the stairs in a cacophony of cracking bones and squishy flesh; bubbles of blood burst in the face and arms, spraying Addison's stilled essence across the stone wall that ran along the stairs. Somewhere in there a finger snagged an errant nail and tore mostly off.

"Shit!" she screamed, realizing she would now have a new enemy to contend with: DNA.

~

How long she watched thick, viscous blood leak from the left side of Addison's skull onto the cement floor at the bottom of the stairs escaped her, but it was long enough for the sun to disappear completely behind the horizon. With lucidity came the realization of the magnitude of the task now before her. With that came tears, and leaving the basement door open, Vicki returned to the small table in the kitchen and wept. She realized with no small amount of anger that Addison was no longer ruining her life, that he had apparently trained her to take over for him in the event of his absence.

"I will not go to jail because of this. I refuse to."

She had to think. She knew she could clean up the blood, but what about the DNA? She'd seen enough forensic television to know blood wasn't the only thing they could use to nail you. Perhaps after she put the body in the furnace, she could walk down to the convenience store at the corner and pick up some bleach and other cleaning supplies? She wanted to google the best way to clean up blood but thought that would be a bad thing if it came to an investigation, which it most certainly would. Shit! Why hadn't she thought about all this before? Several possible timelines branched out in front of her, and every one of them contained an investigation where she was the main suspect. How couldn't she be, the bruised and battered spouse? Vicki realized she would have to take a few days off work - which she couldn't afford to do - but she definitely could not let anyone see her with the black eye and broken nose, the latter of which had begun to throb in low, rhythmic patterns that drew tears from her eyes.

She stood and went back to the top of the stairs. The amount of blood that had now vacated the crack in Addison's skull had created an enormous puddle. She had to act quickly; every second she delayed her task grew. She took the first three steps and stopped cold. She'd seen it clearly enough, the fact that Addison had landed left side down. How was it then that he now lay flat on his back?

"Nope. Uh-ah. No way." She said and commanded her feet to take her down to examine.

They did not oblige.

Something occurred to her. Vicki stormed back to the kitchen, pulled a glass from the cupboard and poured the last third of her beer out where she could see it. Holding the amber liquid up to the light, Vicki tried to analyze the sediment at the bottom of the glass. Again, this wasn't abnormal for a wheat beer. However, another, more sinister idea slipped into place and commandeered the narrative.

Hallucinogens; what if he'd put hallucinogens in the beer?

It made sense that Addison would combine the two things he loved, beer and tripping and that if she'd consumed almost three bottles, she might no longer be able to trust her version of events as they transpired. But there was another voice as well; that part of Vicki's brain that loved horror movies clamored for an attempt at an explanation, offering up an idea she tried very hard to keep from entertaining.

"So which is it, girl? Did Addison put something special in the beer or did he wake up and turn over?"

Neither option seemed particularly appealing.

Vicki returned to sit on the stairs, determined to disprove either theory. She'd just been through a traumatic event at the end of an increasingly traumatic relationship - it seemed only natural her mind would play tricks on her. Ten minutes into her vigil Vicki lapsed into deep thought for an unspecified amount of time and only roused when a sound from the bottom of the stairs stirred her. Her focus returned to Addison's corpse, and staring at it she found she was unsure if another change in position had occurred. The image before her wavered under her drill-bit scrutiny, and as it did Addison's left arm moved ever so slightly.

It was enough to send her into a panic.

"Fuck no!" She screamed as she slammed the door and turned off all the lights in the kitchen. Shaking, Vicki sat staring at the small sliver of light beneath the door, waiting for a shadow to dampen it.

One never did.

The more she thought about it, the more she thought it was likely she'd ingested something that was making her see things. She remembered the story of Addison's that had brought them together, the idea that the hallucinogens had tapped into something primordial in the main character's brain, overhauled his personality in exchange for a more animalistic occupant. This made her think of a story several years ago in the newspaper, a man in Florida eating another man's face. High on a home-brewed hallucinogen, the man did not stop when discovered by police, nor when said cop put a bullet in his arm. It took a second one dead center between the eyes to put him down. An animal? A zombie? Were they the same thing? Had Addison somehow tapped into some-

The front doorbell rang.

"Shit!"

Unsure what to do Vicki snatched the murder weapon off the table and tossed it into the sink, stopped the drain and added a healthy squeeze of dish soap the running water quickly turned into a giant soapy head. Next, she headed out to the living room, inspecting the route for blood. There was a lot.

The doorbell rang again.

"Hold on! Coming. Coming."

She took all of the cushions off the couch and threw them out along the floor, covering most of the blood trail. Then, thinking further into it, she flipped the couch itself over; the commotion brought another iteration of the bell.

"Ready or not."

Just as her hand grasped the doorknob, she remembered the state of her face and froze. As if sensing her proximity a male voice called out from the other side of the door. It was a voice she knew only too well.

"Come on Vicki! Open the fucking door!"

It was Addison's brother Kearn.

"Kearn, I can't."

"What'dya mean ya can't?"

"I... look, Addison and I had a fight. Is he with you?"

"No. Where'd he go?"

"If I knew that I wouldn't be asking if he was with you. The point is he was really mad, and he left and I..." Vicki looked behind her and saw the couch, thought of her face, of Addison's body at the bottom of the basement stairs (hopefully), "I don't want him back here tonight. I'm afraid of him Kearn."

"Well, he ain't with me Vicki so just go ahead and open up."

She hesitated and regretted it immediately. The regret made her reply harsher than it needed to be and that put stress on her narrative.

"Just leave Kearn. You share his blood - I don't want you here either."

"Fucking bitch," she heard him say and then the sound of footsteps down the steps turned her blood to ice. Vicki spun into a mad dash for the back door. Three steps in she collided with the overturned couch, and her momentum sent her face-first into the floor, missing the pillows entirely.

A second later the back door creaked open, and Kearn's voice boomed to her from inside the kitchen.

"Vicki, girl what the hell happened here?"

He came into the room as Vicki picked herself up, eyes wide when he saw the state of her face.

"Your brother happened, Kearn."

He took in the faux devastation of the scene with an uncharacteristic calm. Kearn's anger deflated.

"Jesus Vic, did Addy really do all this?"

"Yep," Vicki answered without hesitation; she knew if she stammered Kearn would see her story for what it was: bullshit.

"I guess I never really wanted to believe you before. You know, about how violent he is."

"It took me a while to believe it too. He's like two different people."

"But, why? I mean, how does that happen?"

"He came into the bedroom the other night, real quiet and afraid. He seemed like the old Addison, you know? He apologized, said the things he did were because of something he couldn't control. That mean anything to you?"

"Not really. But, well, you know how our mom died, right?"

"No, actually I don't."

"She worked in a lab, died from exposure to some chemical. No one ever really told us what it was. Dad disappeared with the insurance check, left me with Addy to take care of, which wasn't as bad as it could have been because we had the house, which was already paid off, and I was old enough to work."

"He never told me any of that. I mean, I knew your mom

had died when Addison was still in high school, but beyond that..."

"You okay?"

"Not really."

They studied one another for a moment, two moons orbiting the same planet from different perspectives. Vicki had once seen Addison the way Kearn did, so she recognized his reluctance to accept the reality. She didn't expect an overturned couch and a bloody lip to persuade him to her cause, but she thought it might at least buy her some time.

A noise from the basement interrupted their moment.

"What was that? He downstairs?"

"He wasn't before."

Even as she spoke, Vicki knew her face betrayed her. She could see suspicion set back into Kearn; the skin around his eyes pulled taut, and the corners of his mouth turned down. She'd almost had him, and now just as quickly she'd lost him.

"Vicki, if you're lying to me there's gonna be a big fuckin' problem."

Before she could respond, Kearn stalked back toward the kitchen. Vicki sucked up the pain in her leg and ran along behind him, grabbed the same knife she'd stabbed Addison with out of the sink as she went. Several steps ahead, Kearn threw open the door and called his brother's name. When Kearn didn't get an answer, he turned back to Vicki, but she had other ideas. Opting against the knife at the last moment, Vicki hit Kearn square in the chest with both hands, her momentum enough to send him head first down the stairs. The problem was, just as he took flight Kearn managed to grasp Vicki by the forearm and that same momentum pulled her out into the open space between the floor and ceiling where she toppled into the abyss beneath her home.

W hen she woke, it was with a sharp stabbing pain in the socket of her right eye. Unable to see clearly or ascertain anything more than the most basic level of her mechanical existence at first, Vicki slowly pulled herself up off the floor and onto her knees. The pain in her eye terrified her, and when she raised her hand to inspect the damage, she had to choke back a tide of vomit when her fingertips discovered what felt like a large splinter jutting out of her eye. Vicki licked her lips and for the second time that night tasted blood. This time though, it was accompanied by a thick, gelatinous residue she instantly equated with the punctured and runny remains of her right eyeball.

"Oh god..." she said an instant before the vomit broke the damn and cascaded from her mouth to the floor. Her left eye blinked in and out, as did her consciousness, and as she fought to stay on her feet, Vicki saw the bile-like yellow of the undigested beer combine with Addison's blood to make a swirling pool of bloody jaundice. It was enough to make her puke a second time before her diaphragm gave out and Vicki collapsed backward opposite the bottom stairs.

Shakey, when she opened her eyes again Vicki saw Kearn lay in a twisted heap across from her, his legs caught up in the open stairs as a pair of tattooed hands clawed at them from the darkness beyond. A low, guttural slathering accented the irregular spasms that wracked the corpse, and as Vicki watched a thick, arterial spray burst through the spaces between the planks and painted the wall next to it in fresh viscera.

She screamed. Behind her, the furnace clicked on, and she ran towards its meager light. To the left of it, she found the door to Addison's office; once inside she threw the lock and put her back against the warped wood, her hands pawing at the wall in search of the light switch. Thwarted by her ignorance of the space Vicki pulled her cell from the back pocket of her jeans; there were cracks in the screen. Holding her breath, her fingertips traced out a familiar pattern and a moment later the flashlight app broke the darkness. The damage had stranded it on the strobe setting, but light was light. The sluggish rhythms painted the tiny space in surrealistic windows, but it wasn't long before she found Addison's desk; if there were any clues as to how this horror had taken root in her life, this is where she would find them. And that's when she saw it.

The book.

In her head, Vicki expected a scene from The Evil Dead - a book bound in flesh and inked in blood, lain open on Addison's desk, the explanation for all of this. Instead, she found... a photo album? Her vision crackled with threats of oblivion but she held on by surprise, leafing through page after page of happy memories - Addison as a child, he and Kearn and their parents. His mother, a beautiful woman who carried in her eyes a gravity unseen in most. Near the end of the book came the pictures of them, of her and Addison, in the earliest days of their relationship.

"This is where I had to come, to stay, to try and fight off what was happening to me. What was always going to happen to me."

His voice surprised her and Vicki turned to see Addison emerge from an unfinished section of the room, where drywall had never been hung. Even in the intermittent light, Vicki could see his face was stained black with gore. Something hung from the corner of Addison's mouth. It looked like hair.

"This is what I am Vicki, what I've always been. I used you to make me better, but it didn't last. She always told me it wouldn't, but I had to find out for myself."

"Your mother?"

"Yes. It was an accident, or rather, an experiment she regretted every day until she died. This curse came to me through her."

"So the Addison I met and fell in love with?"

"An act. The hallucinogens? A convenient cover story to explain my behavior at the height of my sickness."

"And what is your sickness?"

"Flesh. I must have it. I must consume it. I don't know why, but... it's not..."

"It's not your fault?"

"It's not."

A memory of that first night in the gazebo under the stairs broke the surface of her horror, and a deep calm rippled out from around it. Vicki raised her hand and touched the object embedded in her right eye - of course; it was the knife; she'd landed on it. She wouldn't be conscious much longer, let alone alive.

"I'm sorry this happened to you, Addison. I'm sorry it happened to us."

"I'm not. I love you, Vicki. I've always loved you."

Addison opened his arms to her and Vicki moved into his embrace. She swooned when he ran his nose along the nape of her neck.

"Then I am yours."

And once again, in his arms, she felt loved.

MIDNIGHT TREE

It's 2:00 AM, and we're in Sharky's car, speeding north on Cicero towards '55. I'm not really sure what I'm in for here. Sharky's real name is Glenn, and he's head bartender at Manilla's, the restaurant where I recently began working. Apparently, Sharky, or Glenn as I would rather call him just to spite his know-it-all ass, thinks that I've got a whole lot to learn about the bar business, life, women, the whole shebang. I think this because all he does is talk down to me. Not shitty-rich-customer down, but 'yeah, been there, done that, take it from me kid' down. Maybe some people would welcome the advice. Maybe I should welcome the advice, being at a new gig and all. I don't know; I guess it's just my cross in life to bear because I look a lot younger than I actually am. I should be used to it by now but, call me crazy, in this particular situation I have a pretty strong aversion to advice from a guy in a red leather jacket and sky blue loafers.

"Listen, kid; this whole city ain't half a' what it used to be. When I got in on this here gig, this up-all-fuckin'-night, no-bottles-too-dry kinda lifestyle, shit was a hell of a lot different. Look eet, look eet these guys out here!"

We're driving past a gas station at 47th, and there's two dudes in leather jackets out front, one waving his arms wildly while the other one fills up his toy-yellow mustang.

"Motherfuckers like this, you think this kinda' shit rules the night? Naw man, there used to be a kind of ex-cloo-sivity to the wee hours, see? It was all whack-job psychos and drug-fucks. Creatures up and out at this time because what they did wouldn't fly in the light. But now everybody's gone and got themselves a piece of the alternative culture. And see? Everybody out here's an asshole! All the hard crew vampire freaks and blood knuckle fuckers stay in or hit spots guys like you and me'll never know about, right?"

"Heh."

Sharky mistakes my chuckle for amusement and ribs me with his right elbow while skillfully piloting his Buick. Have I gone back in time? Am I about to? We drive on in silence for a few minutes, but I know that won't last. I knew from the second I met Sharky that silence is the one thing he hates more than anything else.

Why?

It threatens his illusions.

"There was this place, back about, oh, I doehn know, maybe twelve years ago, give or take. The Midnight Tree. Dumb name, huh?"

I shrug 'yes' not knowing if this is the correct response.

"I knew the owner; I worked there as a barback, and this guy, Terry Fitzgerald or something, I doehn know, he named it as some kinda stupid puzzle or something. The name was because the place was open every night from midnight to tree, see, so... Midnight Tree? Midnight-ta-tree?"

Oh, I got it all right, Shark. God, I want to kill this guy right now.

"So this place, this place was the fucking place, see?"

"Why?"

There, I spoke.

"At the Midnight Tree the clientele was, ahh, exclusive in that it was anything you wanted. An-ee-thing, but only for those three hours man, only those. Three. Hours."

Wait, what?

"Look, kid, it wasn't always like this. There was sophistication. A danger, see? There was, well, a lot of drugs for one thing."

I give him a humoring-but-frank, 'I know about drugs man, what are you getting at' look.

"Every Friday and Saturday night I ran 'back for this guy Paul, and the thing with this place was we made the money, see? This wasn't so much a bar as it was a den of debauchery. The guy who owned it, Terry what-ever, he had contacts like you wouldn't believe. You name it; coke, tar, hookers, designer shit. It didn't matter. This guy kept us stocked, and on these nights we ran through the stuff, pumping out so much, getting so many people off, it was unreal. And the money? Kid, I'm tellin' you, this was it. I bought my first car while working two nights a week at that place."

This dildo had finally managed to catch my attention. I've heard of this place. Or rather, I've known people who have heard about this place.

"Tell me mor-"

"Well, here ya are kid. Take'er easy."

Of course, just as I'm getting interested, we hit my pad.

"Yeah, you too Shark."

"Eh, I'll take 'er any way I can get'er! Heh, hahhahaha."

One last elbow to the ribs and I'm done for the night. I slam the door to the Buick like it's a Michael Richards mic drop.

~

The following Wednesday I work with Sharky again, and at the end of the night, he's gracious enough to give me another ride. This time though, it's not until halfway home that I get him to start talking.

"That place? That club I told you about last week?"

Yeah, yeah, that's right; Sharky's got a secret. And a good one to boot.

"Forget I told you about it."

"Wait, what? Come on man; you can't do that to me."

"Yeah, uh, look, kid, let's never talk about that place again, okay?"

So what is that? Why bring it up in the first place if he doesn't want to talk about it? Me thinks someone told him to shut his mouth.

Over the next three weeks I pick and chew at the Shark-man for answers or pieces or pieces of answers, but he doesn't budge. What the hell?

Never one to be denied, I start asking around at the bars and clubs I sometimes prowl on the weekend. Trouble is, no one knows anything. Then one night after work, a couple of us from Manilla's end up at this 4:00 A.M. Bar in Stickney, of all places. Stickney - look it up. It looks like a dollop of shit stuck to the map. I usually don't hang out with the folks I work with, but Sharky's here, and he's tying one on pretty good, so this is my chance. I stick to beer and pace myself to make sure I retain control. It doesn't hurt that the only beer they have is Lite, Bud or Special Export - for the fancy pants. Fucking Special Export... exported from where exactly? Nineteen Eighty-Three? Satan's rectum? Ugh, not the most despicable thing I've ever ordered, but close.

Sure enough, by one-thirty Sharky and I are the last two people in the place. Everyone else has either tired of the ashtray ambiance, hooked up or gone off to score drugs at a joint where the bindles served under the counter won't interrupt your run to the bathroom with an actual run to the bathroom. There is however still some staff left, so I wait for Sharky to hit the can and I move us to one of the booths in the back. Don't want anyone hearing what's about to happen.

"Kid? Kid!" Sharky exits the men's room and careens around the room like he just stepped off a tilt o' whirl. I stand up and wave him over.

"What'dya move us fer?"

"Bartender was talking shit."

"Wait? Fug him! I'll fuging' show him…" there it is, the slurring of the speech. It's enough to make the already cloying Chi-town accent sound like it's emanating from behind a mouthful of pizza. Sharky's drunk alright.

Perfect.

While my friend was visiting the little boys' room, I picked up a small sack o' laxative from the door guy, and once I have Sharky situated in the booth I break it out. Sure enough, Sharky sees the drug and his eyes go nuclear. Without so much as a thank you, he snatches the little piece of folded paper from me and starts busting hits off his car keys. I wait for the coke to kick in, wait until he gets that "Ask me a question and I'll be unable to stop answering you" look in his eyes and I not so nonchalantly make my move.

"So, Shark… about that Midnight Tree place."

"Look, kid, I told you I wha-ent gonna talk about thizzhit I know, but see here, thaz because the place is…is dangaross!"

"Yeah, I get that. Keep your fucking voice down, all right Shark?" I tell him, acting all impressed, which of course I guess I really am that someone this low on the food chain knows about a place like this.

"Fug it, ya know? You know there's fugin' real muthafug-gin' vampires? Seriously man. No shit, when I worgded at this fuging place, I saw 'em man. This was some heavy shit, see? Not just drugs but all kind a fuged up shidt, right? I don know man; there was a different time that plast... passed before my eyes an' I don't know who else seen it, but man it was fuging there man."

At this point I don't know what's worse, the Shark-man's alcohol-fueled speech impediment or the circles within which he's talking. My head's ringing and I wish to god I could just close my eyes and be done, but I don't know if I'm going to get another opportunity like this; he's a stream steady flowing, I just have to russet out the gold.

"I godt the job from this guy my cousin knew. She was into a lot of weird shit for a long time before she died, and she got me into some of it too, ya know? Goth, leather, all thadt shidt man. And there was this place on ol' Baldy Avenue, just around the corner from this club where all the spike-heads and fang-fags hung. Ya went into this alley and found this set of old stairs, all totally unmarked, see? And ya only godt in if the guy what answered the door knew your face, and inside... well inside was heaven kid. Heaven..."

What Sharky went on to describe was all too familiar, like something out of a pulp horror rag. A small but well laid-out, two-room cellar converted into the Babylon of the modern world. There was the bar of course, where Sharky ran barback, but along with that there was an in-house connect named Bones that could get you anything you wanted.

Anything.

According to Sharky, this ranged from pot to brown, ladies to babies, guns to fucking ears. The strangest thing Sharky ever saw this Bones guy set somebody up with was a fucking human heart, and according to my new best friend here the recipient wolfed it down in three bites. This is the aforementioned 'vampire' Shark was raving about only moments ago.

Of course, everyone knows better than that. There are no

such things as vampires, sparkly, gothic or otherwise. That said, there are definitely... other things. Nameless things. Nightmare things. And midnight to three? That'd be their prime moving time.

After a while, my questions became less subtle, and even though I know Sharky doesn't want to give up the location that's exactly what he does. That's the thing with most people - the stuff they say they can't tell anyone, even if it's for fear of their safety? They're really just a hop, skip and a jump away from spilling it at any moment. Evolution at work? Maybe. Or maybe it's just the burden of knowledge, and that's all. Either way, you just have to know how to do the asking.

So now I have the inside tip, and I don't mind leaving my unconscious friend alone in this booth, a little trickle of blood running down the side of his face from his nose. I'm going to go back to the pad and rest up because something's telling me Sharky's not going to be at work tomorrow, so I'll get a chance to make some real dough and then head out afterward. Now that I know where the object of my desire is, I need someone who can get me in. Won't be Sharky.

2:00 AM the next night finds me in the western end of the district, hanging out at a goth club called Blood. I'm two big German Weiss beers into a buzz, and I start asking questions. Not many girls in here, so I get the picture, and I start playing the part and batting lashes at the guys who look the most fucked up. One dude's got a King Diamond tattoo side by side with a Reverend Horton Heat one on his sleeveless shoulder, big pink and green spikes rocketing from his noggin and a ripped up Jesus and Mary Chain Tee on, so I'm all over him like glue. I buy him a whiskey and coke and act real impressed that his band, Urine, has an opening slot on tour with another band called Awful Indulgence. Sounds great, eh?

After a time the guy's guard comes down. He's trying to figure out if I'm into him or just a cool one, and, here's the thing about people, they'd rather do something like bust out drugs in front of a stranger and risk possible internment than just ask if they might be interested in a quick one. So now Phil - yeah, that's king punk's name - he's got a key thing going on similar to what Sharky pulled last night, and I'm laughing inside, to myself. Fucking junkies, every last person on the planet it would seem, no?

"So Phil, ah, let me ask thee a question," Phil and I have been joking on the Victorian pastiche that infects every inch of this place for some time now, and I adopt it to get crazy, sexy endearing. I hope. "Is there any place where we can go and get really fucked up together?" He offers the key, but I pass, making it seem like I want to go a couple steps further than just blow.

"Well, I don't know, there's always parties at ..."

"No, no. No, Phi-ill, I'm talking about something like that place that used to be around back in the day. I was only there once, the ahh, the place in the alley...the Midnight Tree."

His reaction shows me that I've hit pay dirt.

"Wow man, you really are in the scene if you know about that fucking place. I was never there, but my bass player and me sometimes party with this guy that used to deal from there."

"Bones?"

"Naw man. Nobody parties with that dude. Not that lives to talk about it, anyway. But he's one'a Bones' couriers. The old place is long gone though. There's a newer place. A pop-up." Phil looks me up and down and then nods, almost to himself, "Shit, you really were there." He's impressed, so I'm in.

Twenty minutes later we're headed to the other side of town where this courier guy hangs and I'm feeling like this could be the real deal. We meet up with him - Andy is this one's name, and I start to wonder about whether or not Phil and Andy are stockbrokers by day - and in a very strange turn of events I know this guy. What's more, he owes me a favor, as I actually drove him to the emergency room once. Long story condensed, there was a party, a fight, and a broken whiskey bottle. Andy shows me he still has the scar on the left side of his back.

"Yeah, okay. I ain't gonna vouch for you with Bones, but I'll get you in. Phil?"

"Na-ah man. I'm out."

Pussy.

No shit. It was that easy. Too bad I can no longer brag to Sharky; my easy access to his fabled club would no doubt drive him insane with jealousy.

We park on Lincoln and head up two blocks, turn into an alley that one hundred percent matches my inner ideal of the place Sharky described to me. There's two large dumpsters and something big scurries around behind them. There's also enough standing water to propagate a cholera outbreak big enough to decimate half the city. Too bad that's not a thing anymore, though if I do meet Bones, maybe I can ask if his range of influence extends to biological compounds.

We go up the stairs - two small flights of old rickety wood that feels like it's going to dissolve beneath my feet at every step - and when we reach the top, a small hatch slides open in the big metal door framed into the side of the building.

"Who the hell's that you're with?" comes a maggoty voice from the other side of the door.

"He was in back in the day, right man?" Andy is trying my patience with his whole approach to living, proactive, as it's left me in a vulnerable spot.

"Yeah, I was at the old Midnight Tree a couple of times back in the day. Never a regular."

"When?"

"When WHAT? What year? I don't fucking know man. About the time Soundgarden broke up, if that helps."

"No, what time were you there? Before or after the midnight crowd let up?"

"Ah, it was all a midnight crowd man, the place was only up from twelve to three, or ah, tree, like that dildo thought he was so clever to name it."

CLIK

A bolt on the door turns, and we're in. Seems like the name's a known joke. Makes me think there's someone bigger paying the bills. Financial backers setting up murder bars that drift on the night, from one spot to another, like the old school raves?

But I'm getting ahead of myself.

Once we're inside, things speed up. There's a table just past the door, and one of the five guys sitting at it is definitely Bones. I know this at first glance.

Of course, Andy sees him and gets visibly nervous; I mean, he's positively shaking. I'll help, even though his discomfort pleases me.

"Better to be on the offensive dude. Introduce me."

"I don't just introduce you to Bones, man. That ain't how it works."

"Is now. You're choice; I don't get in, I run. No one knows me, I'm good. You, they know. If this is a transgression, you're dead."

I feel understanding settle over him like a wet blanket. Smells about the same too. We make our approach and Bones stands. Something flashes in his eyes when he sees me.

"Andrew, how good of you to come. It's been quite some time, yes? Who is your friend?"

"Aww Bones man, you'll dig this. This is Nib. He, ah, he knows you from the old place."

"Realeee…. Nib huh? You do look familiar. But many do." Bones shakes my hand, and I already see the homicidal kind of parasite I'm looking for all over this guy. I'm starting to sweat like this is a *baaaad* idea, but there's no turning back now. Old juices begin to flow, gotta keep my cool and swim in the ocean Andy has just peed for me.

"Yeah, I was there back, fuck, like I told the door guy, around the time my favorite band, Soundgarden broke up. Late nineties? I knew the barback, Sharky."

Blank look. Glenn's nickname's limitations have just shown themselves.

"Glenn, his real name was Glenn."

There is a look of confusion, and then enlightenment as everything apparently plays out for Bones here and complete realization hits him and he sees me for something he hadn't up until a moment ago. Suddenly he realizes why he recognized me from the beginning.

He speaks first.

"Wait a moment, I do remember you. Yes, but it's not from the Tree, no. It's from somewhere else. A party somewhere in…"

"Bucktown, yeah. I thought you looked familiar. I guess you really left your impression on me."

"My dear, I'm quite known for doing that."

We stand, well actually I'm standing but he's sitting, and we just look at each other. That's one thing about this kind of experience; the first time you have it, it never leaves you.

Andy's looking pretty confused and all of a sudden it strikes me, a funny kind of thing to do.

"Hey, Bonesy? Can you get me a human heart by two-thirty?"

"Well my dear," creepy old fingernails gesticulate his words unevenly, "It's been a while since I've fulfilled that particular order. I think, however, I can accommodate you."

Andy's laughing his ass off at this; part of it's discomfort and part of it's not being able to see where this is going at all. Who would?

Bones dips his chin in a gesture that asks "are you sure." I respond by pulling out my wallet. And on that cue Bones' hand is in and out of Andy's chest in the blink of an eye, offering up a fine, if not slightly polluted heart for my approval. Andy - still laughing mind you - just kind of seizes as his blood control center cuts off and sends him to the floor. Now I'm the one laughing, followed by Bones, who reasserts himself and takes my money, only to follow through with a vast, warm hug and a hearty pat on the back.

"Always nice to see someone from the past. Someone who made it through to the here and now without holding a grudge."

"Yeah, I can imagine," I say, wiping blood from my lips, "But Bonesy, who said anything about not holding a grudge?"

With the element of surprise and the adrenaline from taking the heart in two bites, I kill them all easily and without mercy. Ah, blood... When I've finally drunk my fill, I leave the way I came in, taking Andy's car to the neighborhood just outside Midway. Using the cash from the club, I book a flight to the land of long nights in the Northwest, and once there I sleep for a million years, all the while dreaming of murder.

PENTAGRAM GIRLS

The divorce was hard on Gary. He'd come around the curve on the worst of it, the immediate desperation and sadness, but the scar that remained ran deep. The idea that he had wasted eleven years of his life was staggering. Had he actually loved Emily? Of course, it was hard for him to be objective about it now, but the more he thought about it, about those increasingly isolatory years that spanned the gap between meeting Emily to fucking Emily to marrying Emily, the more he became convinced he hadn't stayed with her out of love but loyalty. In high school, a friend once told him, "Loyalty's your weakness dude." Thinking about it on the wrong end of a decade-plus failure, Gary tended to agree.

He had it down as some weird, enigmatic pride that defined that loyalty; pride in being different than the cliche, different than everyone he knew, all the cheaters and philanderers and misogynists. He wasn't sure if this pride stemmed from an insatiable desire to prove something to himself or just everyone else, but either way, it had certainly sent him up the river this time. Alone in the apartment he had shared for the last ten years, Gary found a hole in the center of his existence and wasn't sure how to fill it.

"You need to get laid dude," Graham at work told him during one of their lunchtime philosophy sessions. In hearing the advice, Gary's eyes saucered, as if the idea had never even occurred to him.

"Sex? Hmmm…"

It was in that moment Gary realized that at thirty-four he no longer knew how to meet women.

"Fuck…"

～

"Dating apps man."
To hear Paul say those three words without a hint of irony or humor in his voice made Gary choke on his mouth-full of stout. Paul was sixty-eight and another regular at Shag's Bar, Gary's local haunt. Gary had begun to hit Shag's on an almost nightly basis starting around the time Emily left. In that time he'd befriended exactly two people there: Ribs, the twenty-somethings bartender, and Paul, who according to Ribs had been sitting on the same bar stool for decades. Lost in the entropy generated by an encroaching black hole of despondency, Gary was three pints and two shots into his nightly bender when Paul sauntered in and inquired as to his state.

"Fucked."

"Why?" Paul asked as Ribs placed his customary drink - bourbon and seven - on a napkin before him.

"I don't know how to meet women anymore."

"Then wouldn't you say you're not fucked?"

It took Gary a second to get the joke. When he did, he didn't laugh.

"Oh, come on now Mister sourpuss. It's the twenty-first goddamn century; it's easier to meet women now than any other time in recorded history."

"Oh really?"

"Duh - the fucking internet? Dating apps? Where you been, kid?"

"Married," Ribs said as he crossed by and set three beers out for the squad of female mastodons that had spent the last two hours posing around the pool table.

"Zing," Paul laughed and broke out his phone, leaned over and offered Gary a peek at something on the screen. A red and black heart floated to the top and then opened, revealing a rotating menagerie of pictures, all profiles, all female.

"Crush. It's the bomb."

Ribs nearly spit at that, and one of the girls snarled as she picked up the beers.

"Watch the fucking salvia, jag-off."

"Whatever," Ribs said as she stalked off, tattooed elbows swinging as her friends high-fived her.

"Fucking dike," Ribs said under his breath but still probably loud enough for them to hear. Uncaring, he turned his attention back to Gary and Paul.

"Paul, what the fuck do you know about dating apps man? Aren't you like, a hundred and ten or something?"

Paul stuck his middle finger in Ribs' face and turned back to Gary. He flipped through several pictures until he landed on one of a large-breasted brunette in a skintight leather bra and jeans.

"I'm hitting that."

A beat passed, and then both Gary and Ribs erupted in laughter. It was all a bit much.

"Fuck you guys. I'm twice your fucking age, and I'm doing better than either of you two shits."

"Paul, look at her man. The girls on those things are all whores."

No sooner had he said it then a bolt of bright white lightning collided with the back of Gary's skull and he went down. Reality skipped a beat, and when it resettled, he found himself on the floor, staring up at one of the mastodons, the pool cue in her hand cracked into jagged teeth from where she had just broken it over his head.

"I met my fucking boyfriend on one of those apps you pig."

Surprised, Gary raised a hand as a pacifying gesture and tried to offer an apology but before he could utter a word another of the girls stepped forward and spat directly in his face.

"Jesus Christ! I'm sorry, okay? I was just trying to-" now the third in the group joined in, and before he knew it Gary was running from Shag's, a giant globule of saliva still hanging from his left cheek, a surrogate for the tears he wanted to cry at his increasingly depressing existence.

∾

Back at his place, Gary cracked a sixer of expensive IPA he stopped off at the gas station for and let Aleister out of her terrarium. At nearly six feet in length and twenty-seven pounds, Aleister was considerably larger than Gary had ever heard of a pet Python growing. He'd upsized her quarters twice and was anticipating a possible third, which would be expensive. Gary didn't mind though. After all, the snake was the only one who had stayed with him unconditionally.

"Long day Ali," he said as he sat down on the floor by the coffee table and watched the thick, muscular form slowly unwind; watching the snake move Gary never ceased to feel awe at its elegant design. He wished he could be as strong and flawless, but watching Aleister glide across the hardwood floor in slow motion, Gary knew the truth. He was no snake.

"That's my fucking problem."

He finished half the beer and then opened his laptop, typed in the address of the dating website he'd tried briefly before he met Emily, back when online dating was a considerably more novel thing. After a few moments of trying to remember his password, he realized his mistake.

"It's all mobile now stupid."

Curiosity renewed, he snatched his phone off the table and double-tapped the App store icon; sure enough, there in the top sellers was Crush. Sixty-fucking-eight-year-old Paul, a man twice his age schooling him on dating apps.

"Fucking pathetic."

Gary downloaded the app.

Sixty-three seconds later he typed his email into the username field and created a password. The little green wheel appeared and traveled around and around for several moments before - girls.

Lots of girls.

One hand on his second beer, Gary used the other to scroll through profile after profile of single women, their likes and preferences listed below snapshots taken in front of the mirror, in bathing suits, in pick-up trucks, in the bathtub, in...

In the center of a pentagram?

"What. The. Fuck."

He couldn't look away. The girl was gorgeous, and what's more, she seemed to offer an antidote to the boring, missionary existence he'd led for so long. Looking further he discovered her name was Taylor; Gary immediately swiped his way toward an introduction. Afterward, his session felt spent; he continued to browse but with considerably less enthusiasm. He'd found the girl he wanted to talk to. Unfortunately, no response came, not in ten minutes, not twenty. Three hours later Gary was passed out drunk on the living room floor, the last beer in the six pack warming on the carpet beneath him.

~

Taylor never did respond, but by the time Gary woke up hungover and out of sorts the next morning he saw he had several responses from the girls he'd 'liked' before seeing her. He didn't know what to say. Paul had been right. Sixty-eight-year-old Paul had saved his ass.

Gary put on a pot of coffee and began to read through the messages, formulating as genuine a response as he could to each one.

~

He couldn't say where it'd come from or how, but by November it'd been six months of non-stop savior faire for Gary. And now it was over. Boy was it over.

It started with a case of mistaken identity and the girl in the bookstore. They'd each 'liked' one another's profiles, then chatted a bit through the app. Both were fans of late 70's Post Punk, and that was his in. Gary had let Jody come around to the idea of meeting, and when she did, her suggestion suited him just fine - the cafe inside the local Boundaries Bookstore. He'd arrived early intending to bolster his self-esteem with copious amounts of caffeine but spotted her the moment he walked through the door: a cute little number with red hair and long legs that dripped black denim, a faded Joy Division t-shirt her identifying trait. He approached and offered a confident but not cocky hello, immediately commenting on how much he liked her shirt. And the funny thing was, as he spoke Gary could hear himself, and he didn't sound anything at all like what he was used to hearing. He sounded interesting, self-assured and even a skosh debonair. His words came out strong and interesting, descriptors confirmed by the smile and interest exhibited on their intended recipient's face. He asked to sit, and it only took a few more moments for him to realize two important things. One, it wasn't just his words, it was the sentiment behind them; Gary spoke like he felt; curious, confident and, honestly, a touch predatory. And two, this wasn't the girl from the app. This was someone else, a random coincidence that he should show up and meet a second girl into one of his favorite bands at this apparent nexus of culture. What were the odds?

The girl's name was Beth, and after that first fateful meeting they'd gone out a handful of times and then she'd unceremoniously informed him in a text that he shouldn't call anymore, that she was getting back together with her ex. Gary read the message, and another extraordinary thing happened.

He didn't care.

Next, it was Cora. They went out twice, had sex the second time and then it just never happened again, as though it'd run its course. But by then he had invitations piling up; without batting an eye he met Christy, they dated three times, kissed once and then he met Nancy. And then Kaitlin. And then another Beth. And then…

Nothing. Just as quickly and unlikely as it had begun, Gary's winning streak turned south. Two months on he'd not been on a date since Beth Number Two.

"Aleister, what the fuck am I going to do?"

The snake did not answer.

~

When he went to sleep that night, Gary dreamed dark, disturbing dreams about, of all things, meat. Thick, bloody slabs of beef, spread out all over some enormous room's endless counter space. In the dream he was hacking through a tough portion of what looked like pork shoulder, a great joy overwhelming him as he prepared a celebratory meal. Analyzing it later, Gary thought he remembered Aleister coiled on a massive chair, her neck raised so high above a carved wooden table she looked like a Matriarch presiding over a family meal. The snake expected to be fed, but try as he might Gary could not hack through the thick, marbled muscle.

~

Looking back on his dating ups and downs, Gary couldn't help but think there was some unconscious button the app had switched on and that somehow, after only a few months, he'd accidentally managed to switch it back off. The proficiency he had begun to take for granted became a daily horror show: harsh, demeaning efforts where at best he heard "No" and at worst "creep" or "cops." Was he ever out of line? Gary didn't think so. But he also figured that, after a while, his lack-of-mojo became an exponential snowball that left the rank stench of desperation seeping through his clothes, his hair, from every pore on his body. He'd gone from awkward, to married, to secure, to devastated, to pimp, to…

"Inert gas," he said as he farted into the carpet and stood

to get another beer. Aleister was out and heading toward the radiator, but it'd be a moment before she got there so, buzzed, Gary let her go, stood up and walked to the kitchen where he pulled another beer from the fridge, thought about it and then pulled two more.

"Why get back up?"

He pulled the brass church key from the top drawer in the white Formica countertop, opened the beers and then returned to the living room where he settled back into his spot on the floor, Aleister on the coffee table this time, uncoiling slowly toward the carpet. The snake looked noticeably bigger than yesterday...

"How'd you get up there that fast, Ali?"

The snake did not answer.

$\sim$

After yet another disastrous attempt at speaking to a girl - this one while shopping at the Whole Paycheck down the street from his house - Gary returned with a fresh sixer and a newfound determination to solve his problem.

"Alright, let's just fuckin' see about thish..." Gary drunkenly opened Crush and began to swipe, a half-formed strategy floating around his increasingly fevered search. Then, five minutes or so later, there she was.

Pentagram girl - Taylor. He almost missed her at first, as she'd changed her profile. The pentagram picture was still there, but so were several more innocuous photos - one taken at a lake on a sunny day, one in someone's wood-paneled basement or attic, horror movie posters on the walls and green Christmas lights strung from the ceiling. And, incredibly, one of her in a red hooded robe, a curved dagger in her left hand. The robe fell open down the center in a way that you could just begin to see the outward curves of her breasts, a nipple dancing at the very edge of the fabric.

"Holy shit."

~

The strategy, as all strategies born of drunken desperation, was admittedly stupid. But it came from a place of hope and for Gary that was a novel thing at the moment, so he went with it. Determined, he finished another beer and fired up his laptop.

SEARCH: Satanic Rituals

RESULTS:

"Interesting..."

~

Two days later his research had become a black hole. Beginning with Wikipedia, Gary spiderwebbed through dozens of linked articles, all branching off of the occult. One of the first things he learned was the symbol he had mistaken for a Pentagram was actually a deviation of the ancient symbol, one that appeared to have no specific name but was linked to - of all things - an ancient cult that dated back to Mesopotamia. This cult's major deity was a Snake God with an unpronounceable name most people online shortened to "K'or."

"See Ali!" he slurred at the snake while he read, "This chick worships snakes. And I've got you... how can she not like me?"

Gary immediately constructed a new profile, the main picture of which featured Aleister swaddled tightly around his neck.

The snake had definitely put on weight.

Not twenty minutes after he posted the new profile - careful to remove the old one of course - Gary received a 'Wink' from Taylor.

"Yes!" he screamed at the top of his lungs. Aleister regarded him from a place across the room, quiet and contemplative as usual.

～

The dream returned that night, louder and more vivid than before. In it Gary continued to hack at the same piece of curmudgeonous meat, the countertop before him saturated with blood and chunks of flesh. Frustration mounting, Dream-Gary turned the meat over to get a better angle with the blade and for the first time saw K'or's symbol carved into the workspace. The recognition felt as though it empowered him, and when he went back at it, the meat practically melted with the first new strokes of the blade. As the sinew parted and the muscle divided he saw something else he had not noticed before.

The meat had what looked like a tattoo.

～

The anxiety Gary had anticipated leading up to meeting Taylor never manifested; instead, he found his spirits once again high and his self-esteem back in the stratosphere. They met in a coffee shop that she suggested; it wasn't far from his place, so Gary knew it well. He arrived early and stood when she entered, recognizing her immediately; her hair extensions, threaded eyebrows, and a menagerie of piercings stood out like a beacon in the sea of stagnant Gen Xers that usually frequented the place. She sat, and when Gary asked what she wanted she answered that she'd already

ordered via a mobile app. Once situated, they fell into immediate conversation; she asked him briefly about his marriage,
his job, his taste in music and, of course, his snake.

"Her name's Aleister."

"Cool. I love snakes."

"I gathered that from your profile."

"You did?"

"I researched you a bit."

"Really?" Taylor cocked her eyebrow and smiled at that.
Gary had hoped she would take it for what it was: flattery.

"And what did you find?"

"I read about K'or and the people who worship her, it,
whatever."

Taylor laughed, and Gary felt as though he had scored
enough points to advance the game.

"You wanna see my snake, Taylor?"

Her smile widened.

"I do, Gary."

～

Watching Taylor handle Aleister was a strangely
erotic thing. The snake seemed to feel immediately
comfortable with her, something that had never been true
with Emily.

"She likes you."

"Of course. She's my god."

"Haha."

"No, seriously. In K'oratelan philosophy, all snakes are
vessels for K'ortelash's spirit."

"That's awesome. What made you turn to K'ore… K'ortl…
to this particular philosophy?"

"I had an experience that changed my life. It involved a
snake, and it led me to do reading, same as you. The more I

read, the more I realized I wasn't reading a philosophy but a cosmic truth."

"That's pretty deep."

"KP - that's what I call it for short - is just as valid a religion as anything Mom-Middle school teaches her fucking American Nightmare children. Snakes get a bad wrap because of the Bible, and the Bible ascribes them a relationship with knowledge - knowledge that is somehow "evil." Think about it, Adam and Eve are cold and stupid in the garden, the Serpent shows up and says, hey guys, um, you know you don't have to walk around naked and oh, by the way, here's a new way to look at things and BOOM! He's the bad guy. Kinda seems like their god wants his children to be stupid, doesn't it?"

"Wow. I never thought about it like that before."

"Of course you didn't - you've been programmed like everyone else."

Gary winced at the condemnation.

"I didn't mean it as an insult; I was like you once too. I mean, I know that sounds like I have a superiority complex but, well, I kinda do," she said and smiled.

"No, no you're right. I mean, that's what drew me to you - I've lived my life the way I thought I was supposed to, the way I was essentially told to for over three decades and well, doing so has left me broken and alone."

"Easy Trent Reznor," She said and laughed to let him know it was camaraderie, not criticism.

"Right."

"So how long were you with her?"

"Emily? Eleven years total, ten married."

"One year before tying the knot? Jesus, I hope you learned your lesson on that one."

"Yeah. I don't know what I was thinking at the time. I mean, there were… circumstances."

"Kids?"

"Hell no."

"Another plus."

"You?"

"Fuck no. I had my tubes tied at nineteen. I hate the little fuckers."

"Me too. I've got Aleister, that's enough. Hey, um… can I…"

"You want to ask me about the pictures on my profile?"

"I do."

"Did they scare you?"

"What do you think?"

"I think I never realized how many averages Joe's fantasize about fucking a girl on a sacrificial altar."

"Is that what that was? A sacrificial altar?"

"In a way."

"That symbol… I mistook it for a pentagram until I started reading about K'or. Now, well, would you believe that I've started seeing it in my dreams?"

"Gary, that's wonderful. That means She has chosen you."

"K'or?"

Taylor nodded and whispered something to Aleister. The snake coiled tighter around her. It looked like it was hugging her.

"Dreams can come true you know."

"I don't know about this one-"

Taylor shushed him and drew closer.

"Do you want to know how to change your life, Gary?"

"More than anything."

"Come here."

Still holding Aleister, they moved into an embrace and before he realized what was happening the snake slid from Taylor's shoulders to his. Its tongue probed Gary's ear as

Taylor's hand moved down to caress the encroaching bulge in his jeans.

"Let us pray."

~

Three weeks went by and Gary and Taylor entered into the most unique relationship he could have imagined. Whenever he tried to call or message her, she didn't respond. But every third night Taylor would knock on his door just before he went to sleep. He'd answer, and she'd come in, and they'd go straight at it, fucking like there was no tomorrow, the snake always out of the terrarium, moving around them, its hiss a constant soundtrack to their formidable coupling.

~

On three month anniversary of his first meeting with Taylor, Gary woke in the morning with the most vivid impressions from the recurring dream yet. This time the meat had revealed more than just a tattoo. Arranged on the countertop with K'or's symbol were what looked like human limbs, the flesh, and bone at the ends torn and ragged. Nearby a nested, fibrous material floated in a pot of boiling water. It looked like hair. Strangest of all, from somewhere in the distance Gary thought he heard... the Allman Brothers?

~

The phone call surprised him.

"Gary. Can we talk?"

"Jesus Christ Emily. Do you know what fucking time it is? I've got work in the morning."

"I know, I just... I'm in trouble."

'Here it comes,' he thought and in spite of his annoyance smiled, 'This is where she tells me my replacement beat the shit out of her, or fucked another chick, or robbed a bank; nothing would surprise him at this point.

"Are you okay?"

"Yeah, if you count being locked out of my place okay."

"Did you and Cunty get into a fight?"

"It's... he hit me, Gary. I came home and found some other girl in the house, and he acted like it was no big deal, you know? He tried to play it off like nothing had happened, said she was just a neighbor. But-"

"A neighbor huh? She's from the neighborhood?" the reference made him smile even if it was wasted on Emily.

"Yeah, ah, I guess. But I knew... and then when I confronted him, he told me to fuck off. I pay the rent, and I told him to get out and..."

"I don't need all the fucking details. Where are you?" Gary asked, a voice in his head already chastising him for not hanging up. As she spoke his attention waned; Taylor was asleep beside him, and Aleister sat coiled in the chair across the room, her long, muscular body unraveled at the top, her head the same height as Gary's. She looked so human, regarded him with a look he had seen somewhere before. It gave him chills, the way the snake held his eye contact.

"Gary? Are you still there?"

"Look, Emily, get to the fucking point. What do you need?"

"I need a place to stay Gary."

"Are you fucking serious?"

"Oh, sorry to interrupt your sitting around getting drunk or stoned or whatever. I'll just stay out here and end up dead."

Aleister's expression changed, and Gary jumped when he

felt something move along his inner thigh. He looked down and saw Taylor, awake.

"Invite her to stay," she mouthed.

"Are you serious?" he asked. Emily thought he was talking to her.

"How many times are you going to ask me that? Yes, I'm serious. This is life or death, Gary."

Taylor nodded again, her hand moving further up his thigh.

"Yeah. Yeah, okay."

"Really?"

"Yeah. How long until you get here?"

"Well, Rex has my car too so I thought maybe you could…"

"You thought I'd drive three and a half hours out to the desert to pick you up? Jesus fucking Christ Emily."

"It's fine. We'll pick her up," Taylor said, her head in his lap. She stopped talking.

"Yeah, uh, okay. Text me the address."

Gary hung up.

$\sim$

The unreality of the situation kept Gary quiet for the first hour of the drive. After that, however, something popped and he had to know.

"What are we doing Taylor? Why did you tell me to let her stay?"

"Don't ask. Just let it happen."

"Let what happen?"

"Transformation."

Taylor reached forward and turned on the stereo. Some metal song Gary didn't recognize came through from the left of the dial, intermittent packets of static ruffling the song's edges, playing games with its slow, sludge-like march. In the rearview mirror, the sun eased its way below the shimmering edge of the horizon, its rays turning the road purple and black ahead of them. Gary searched his thoughts for some clue as to what he was doing, why he was doing it. There were none, and for the next forty minutes, the sludge metal opus drawled thick crimson slabs through an increasingly erratic storm of static. Outside, the stars winked into view in gobs. Beside him, Taylor became focused on her phone. After a few minutes, she held it out for him to look at it. There was an image on the screen Gary had seen before.

"Do you know what this is Gary?"

Gary took his eyes off the road for a single instant; seeing the picture, something in the pit of his stomach awoke and sought to see the world through his eyes.

"What the fuck is that?" he said, pinning his eyes back on the road. Taylor held the phone steady for a moment, but he kept his eyes as far from it as possible. Despite his inability to process - let alone describe - the image on the screen, he could feel it working through his brain. The thing in his stomach tugged at his eyes until it became impossible to ignore. He sought the image once again and a calm settled over him.

"That Gary, is the future. Your future. Our future."

An image of Aleister came unbidden into his head, and Gary suddenly realized he knew exactly what the picture was. Correction: What it would be. The realization hit him just as Gary turned the car off the main road and he saw Emily standing before a pink and white double wide with a garish American Flag hung across the space between the two front windows. She stood in front of the structure, Cunty in the open doorway, no shirt on, a faded Allman Brothers tattoo covering most of his chest.

"Oh sure. Here's this fucking dickhead," he shouted at

Gary as he put the car into park. "You come to take your fucking bitch back? Like ta see you try amigo."

Cunty descended the three dilapidated iron stairs in a quick burst and puffed up his chest in a territorial declaration. His skin was tight and leathery, like George Hamilton on a grill. Gary watched the ex-hippy's sad pomp and circumstance and felt uncompelled. He realized now that he didn't care at all what happened to this person, to either of these people.

Then he realized that was a lie. He did care. In Gary's head, the image from Taylor's phone took its rightful place in the continuity of his recurring dream. Everything aligned for him now: a bloody slab of raw, red meat choked with maggots and barbed wire; a large butcher's knife buried to the hilt, and a certain threatening geometry where the hard-line bisected the soft, spongy texture of life in all its frailty.

Gary popped the trunk and rolled down the window. His eyes went from Cunty to Emily.

"Get in."

Emily stood aghast at the sight of Taylor in the passenger seat.

"Who the fuck is she?"

Taylor was out of the car so quickly Gary didn't even realize it was her in front of the windshield. The sound of a gunshot pulled a black sackcloth over his ears and left a heinous ringing behind. On the metal steps, Cunty crumpled like dirty laundry and Gary began to laugh.

"Oh my god!" Emily screamed, and before he knew it, Gary was on her, pulling a towel he'd not even realized he was holding over her head and driving his fist into her temple several times in a row. When it was over and she was unmoving Gary looked to Emily, who stood smiling at him.

"Do you feel it, Gary? Do you feel the transformation taking place?"

SHAWN C. BAKER

"I do," he said, moving to her and swallowing her tongue, moving his hand along her cool, white thigh.

"Do you want to fuck me on your ex-wife's corpse?"

"I do."

"Then let's get them in the trunk. And Gary…"

"Yeah?"

"I told you dreams could come true."

1422 EUCLID

"Slake the thirst."

He woke in the early morning, paralyzed by the remaining tendrils of the dream. As they slithered out the back door of his mind, flushed from his consciousness like waste down a storm drain, Drew re-experienced the images and found they were the same. They were always the same. And despite the fact that it had been awhile since the last iteration of this nightmare, he recognized it wholeheartedly and, what's more, now felt foolish he'd ever considered it conquered. With this evening taken as a fresh assault, his brief respite now seemed less a reprieve than a tactic for the dream to increase its impact. And what did that say, the idea that his own mind had leveraged itself against him?

Nothing good.

Two years rehabilitation and Drew could feel the façade beginning to slip. He'd been low at the end. Low enough to recognize the view again now, to remember the smell of his own tainted flesh as it crawled with the bugs of compulsion, seething with the flavor he woke choking on in the middle of the night. Hot, musky and sharp, it cloyed incessantly in the back of his throat, overpowering but never quite strong enough.

Never *realized*.

He remembered that flavor now – tasted it on the back of his tongue, in the depths of the dream – and wished for it once more.

"Slake the thirst."

This was the copy in the ad that caught his attention, a brevity in the back of a skin mag; a slogan that would somehow not let go. "Slake the thirst," the magazine said, and it was those same three words the voice on the other end of the telephone said to him now.

"What did you say?" he asked, certain he'd imagined it.

"You've been away for a long time, haven't you? What is your name child?"

"Drew," he had no idea why he would answer a question like that in a situation such as this. "What did you say, a minute ago?"

"You must have built up quite a thirst Drew. We aid people like you. People who have acquired certain... appetites."

The voice was familiar.

'It can't be,' he said to himself, just shy of out loud. It couldn't be, but with each passing second, Drew became sure it was. The strange, alternately masculine/feminine cadence; the rich, syrupy lilt of the A's and the E's. That was all he could think while the cold plastic of the phone began to warm against his ear, the bridge that presented this new opportunity to him. A bridge to something he'd thought he had left behind. Something he thought he'd escaped.

They had found him. *He* had found him.

"It's a long, cold slide to the depths of hell," Drew muttered, consonants sticking against the back of his throat.

"That's not true at all Drew. You know it's not. A long slide yes, but it's warm, and moist, and filled with all manner of wonderful friction."

"I've... I... I'm recovered."

"Recovery is a lie Drew. There is only one time, one outcome. You cannot escape what you are. Your new life is a fraud; this is the voice of your old life. Your *real* life."

It was him, Drew was sure of it. On the other end of the line: Mr. Brittany. Drew's skin began to crawl with the memory of the awful things he had done in the presence of this person. The awful things he wanted to do again.

"Do not deny the time you have left on this Earth, Drew. Once it has passed, so too will these secrets pass beyond your reach. You have tasted the blood and glimpsed what lay beyond the stars. You know that there is more to experience than just the world of man."

"How did you find me?" he shrieked, almost in tears.

"Oh but Drew, you found me, remember?"

Instruction received, remember he did.

~

Drew had gone through a twelve-step program. He'd gotten lost just twice, near the beginning. But sex proved to be like cigarettes – there was no occasion to it. No special celebrations or even normal, healthy relationships. Those things only re-introduced the temptation and brought the dreams; the dreams where one thousand hands smoothed and cupped him, circled and milked him.

The albatross had first appeared while he was teaching at the University. The doorway opened in the form of a young co-ed named Faye who had a proclivity for her professors and group, ritualistic sex. Frightened at first, Drew soon found that the fear engaged him; it enhanced his experience in a relationship already secretive and dangerous. Through Faye, he attended gatherings where the floors of mansions, churches, and mausoleums writhed with scores of naked participants, all locked in perpetual spasm; bodies that had become single cells in something far greater than just lust, fueled by a power frightening and yet beautiful in its primitive simplicity. It was here, in these buildings, on these floors, where Drew first felt the eyes of something more significant than the world he knew, where he first became aware of something Other watching him. Acknowledging him.

From there Drew's world became eclipsed by something darker. He was welcomed into a dimension of frenzy and privilege, compulsion and need. A need to obliterate his flesh; to slip behind his conscious mind for a glimpse of that presence. What was it like? Hostile? Loving? He didn't know, but it was all he could think about. He'd shined a light into the darkness and crossed paths with something ineffable. Something omnipotent.

Moving quickly from fledgling to host, Drew began to entertain small parties at the cabin on the lake he'd inherited from his Aunt. Previously he'd never found a use for the place, but now its simple structure - a mere two rooms with no amenities - became his sacred space. The main room – called the 'great room' since before Drew was born – was traditionally the location of the rites. The adjoining bedroom then was a small enclave of privacy to be utilized for whatever conceivable private matters a person might require at an orgy. The entire structure was a rapidly declining eighteenth-century wood, perhaps Hemlock Fir, and it culminated with a small, lakeside porch that time and the surrounding forest had finally swallowed whole sometime during the previous decade. The effect of the entire tableau was raw and dying as residences go, and yet morosely charming at the same time.

Word spread amidst the circle of charlatans and freaks that comprised their loosely knit society, and soon Drew's audience grew. He wasn't ready for that. The mechanics of these functions required space, and as time went by, they ran out of it. Often, on warmer nights, the festivities began to spill over to the outside. Friends and strangers copulating beneath the stars, fucking like their primitive ancestors in the woods, by the lake, seeking the approval of the distant, fiery gods that winked down at them from millions of miles away, each one a celestial body that no longer existed by the time their approval arrived. It was here that Drew first felt the presence speak to him. One word, real or imagined:

"Thirst."

The word triggered an image in the back of his mind: a contortionist. No, that wasn't quite right. Drew could feel the image as a physical presence more than he could see it. Something... unnatural. Something... blasphemously erotic.

He redoubled his efforts, took frightening risks, all to extend the conversation.

Then one night Faye caught something, a bug of doubt or a morsel of faith – he wasn't sure which – and defected back to her surprisingly tame suburban beginnings.

Drew found himself alone and unsteady in his own creation.

He tried to curtail the festivities, but by then, even without invitation, people still came from far and wide for the chance to take part in what had become something of an underground phenomenon. When asked, many of Drew's regular guests explained they had found a connection in *that* house, on *that* lake, surrounded by *that* forest. Something about the combination of picturesque beauty, ancient décor, and Drew's own maddeningly intoxicating dedication made it, to quote one man Drew interviewed on the subject, 'An ally.'

Not a good thing.

The situation escalated. Strangers he was sure he hadn't hosted previously would appear at all hours, leaving notes, phone numbers, and addresses when he was not there. At first, Drew tried to stay away himself, bury his longings with the cleansing of daily rituals: work and routine, cities and light. But that maddening brush with the ineffable and the unquenchable thirst it had awakened was always near; it strobed in the corner of his eye and woke him with hushed whispers in the night. His daily life ground to a halt and soon he found he could stay away no longer, the compulsion was too great.

He began to live at the cabin.

From there, the end. Drew's job suffered. His relation-ships died. By forsaking his friends and career in favor of his role as den mother, Drew slowly closed the book on who he had been and became something else: a living, breathing need; an impulse that his entire existence revolved around answering, despite the fact that the language that dressed it was incomprehensible to a mind so full of self-deceit.

Months passed. Things began to take on a sick shade of desperation, and what had started as curiosity turned, inevitably, to sustenance. And then one night a representa-tive of that Other came to him, and everything Drew had ever been drowned in the deepest shades of crimson.

Death made its presence known to him then, and in his sick and filthy little heart, Drew considered them well-met.

Even as it happened, Drew understood that this was the next logical step on the path he had opened for himself. It had been hard to pull back, at the end, and it had left him destitute; he only spent two years in prison due to a techni-cality but was cast out of the University and lost everyone around him who mattered. For ten dollars and seventy-five cents an hour, Drew took a job at a hospital, sweeping up sick and hosing down body bags. Most days it disgusted him. On others, it felt as close as he could safely get to what he wanted most: to feel the veins of life seize in his presence, to taste the flavor of pitch-black death, an acknowledgment that the Presence was there with him, in spirit if not in flesh.

Despite the appetite awakened in him, Drew remained haunted by the things he'd taken part in. Often, when he least expected, he relived parts of that night in violent, almost epileptic flashes that played the images from the cabin fresh across his mind. Two girls, the man – Mr. Brittany – a distinguished, serpentine brooder with a glint of evil in his eye and the smile of a minister. Drew had heard of him, had even played at attracting him with his parties. He was almost more myth than reality, like the Candy Man who appeared when his name was invoked before the mirror. Only Mr. Brittany was very much real, and once he arrived, he stayed with Drew forever after.

But that's wrong, his use of the word 'arrived', because Mr. Brittany had *always* been there. It was as if it was Drew who was a guest in his world, not the other way around. Mr. Brittany, harbinger of something grander, had merely been waiting for the right moment to make his presence known. And when he did, he did so with a familiarity and grace that made him feel like an old friend. Accordingly, he brought some of his own friends with him as well. One of these friends was a girl who turned out to be a runaway from a mental institution. Had Drew known then what he would learn later... no. He couldn't fool himself; it would not have mattered.

The four of them went at it, presided over by Brittany's strange liturgy, words of ill-syllable and sickening cadence that resounded throughout the entire event. Fucking, casual violence, the lines between pleasure and pain blurred and as they did a new and sickly worldview encroached. Mr. Brittany asked Drew if he had ever tasted human blood. The answer – no – seemed to put Drew at a disadvantage. He became ashamed, disjointed. "Not to fear, there is a first time for everything," Mr. Brittany remarked casually. And then there was a knife in his hand, in Drew's hand. Mr. Brittany smiled. The room ran red, urges spilled over into one another and... Drew remembered the feeling of life running through his fingers, coating the back of his throat. It both excited and sickened him still. It was the taste.

The taste that slaked the thirst.

There were appetites he'd not known existed, and these terrible people had awakened them inside of him. They had initiated him; opened him. The ejaculate of death was every bit as sweet as that of life, and the spiral that appeared around its edges - his edges - took every last ounce of Drew's strength to pull himself back from and finally seek help.

Months passed, thirty-three to be exact. It was a struggle. Drew had his meetings, his sponsor Gail. She cared about him; cared what happened to him because, as she said, "We all deserve a second chance." To her face Drew thanked her and agreed, but at night, when he was alone and the memories of cutting the girl's throat came to him, he wasn't so sure. The way even in her death throws she (he didn't remember her name, didn't know if he'd ever even known her name to begin with) smiled and presented herself to him, handing her life over with just one word:

"Drink."

And drink he did, to alleviate the thirst. Mr. Brittany offered the blood to Drew in an onyx-studded chalice, a black mass communion, the pounding of unknown pleasures awakening within him, pulling him by the back, the shoulders, the sex until he had at last quaffed of the unholy imbibe... the corpse so warm. It was in these moments that Drew hated Gail and her second chances. In these moments he sought his own destruction to quell the building reservoir he feared would one day burst. He held his own quiet little vigil – when the thoughts came, he took a straight razor and cut a swath of flesh away and waited for the dark energies to leave him. He was a medieval priest, puncturing peoples' skulls to cure them of the demons science would one day call epilepsy. He was a nineteen-thirties quack using leeches to fight cancer. And when the bleeding was not enough, he would cauterize the wound with a hot piece of iron in the shape of a cross he'd taken from off his wall decades before, reveling in the smell of his smoldering skin. Then it was into the night to do the only other thing he could think to do: find a bar and drink. Drink away the thirst.

But it was never the right flavor.

~

As he stepped through the door to his apartment, Drew found for the first time these memories felt like glorifications. He would try to drown them one last time; he was slipping, had to try to turn it around.

In his head something crackled; an 8-bit image of... what? Something so familiar. A spider? A crab? A...

Contortionist?

He blinked and realized he was already at the bar, as though he had stepped through a portal. Drew's surrender to memory had escalated of late, so quasi-fugue states were not uncommon. This, however, this was something different altogether. He'd opened the front door of his apartment, moved to the stairs and immediately found himself descending a dark and dingy staircase into the strobing red lights of a fetish club. Just like that; no memory of the journey, no warning he was about to fall off the wagon. From the mildewed, mid-twentieth century SRO-style environment of his current, pathetic home into the smoke and stink of a rancid fog machine. There had been no interruption in either time or space; one location had simply bled directly into the other.

He paid his money to a man in a black leatherette with scars across his face and track marks up and down his bare arms. He entered and the constant, saw-toothed whine Drew had grown so accustomed to since his rehabilitation became louder than it had ever been. Louder, and more intense; a warbling, arpeggiated throb of wanton desire that matched the syncopated industrial rhythms and remorseless narcissism on display all around him. Empowered yet paralyzed at the same time, Drew took a deep breath and felt the malevolent power of the world he had tried to deny as it enveloped him once more.

"What do we have herrrreeeeee," the question a dark, fibrous hiss issued from a strange and elastically strident form that had emerged behind him. Humanoid, it leered and sniffed at Drew, drawing imaginary circles of ownership up and around his back, his shoulders, a stray finger brushing the cusp of his thigh. Intrigued and aroused, a geyser of ancient waters awakened within him and spurred Drew to action. He caught the rhythm, traced and fondled the androgynous shape with his eyes. Leather from head to toe as it circled and examined him, drinking Drew with invisible eyes.

The first stray sparks of ecstasy caught as he fell into the negative space of the stranger's embrace. Drew circled his head through the same routine, bent and twisted his back low and around to match the sanguine orbit offered him. He dipped his shoulders to keep up, the music beginning to move him into some freak tribal maneuver born of the ancient world. They circled each other like lovers, or prey, or lovers wont to prey on one another; pieces of the ancient world where this was all there was to live for. No money, no automobiles, no television. No universities and no education that you didn't learn from doing first hand. No pain; no pleasure that wasn't born of or connected to the timeless cycle of life and the one immediate need that trumped all others:

Drop to the field before you and plant your seed.

Their paths eventually put them face to face. Drew's visage was unobscured, but the stranger wore the mask with the infamous zipper for a mouth, a filter for a poisonous hole. Drew altered his rhythm proportionately, sent his arm rippling toward the object of his desire. They made eye contact, and everything stopped.

Dead.

The ceiling of the world collapsed. Suddenly the music was too loud, the lights were too low and Drew could hear Gail screaming in the back of his head, screaming about second chances and damnation and the slippery slope to hell. He remembered when she had first agreed to be his sponsor she'd had a moment of weakness herself. At that moment their roles had reversed, and she'd looked at him so severely that inside her eyes Drew thought he'd recognized the distant reflections of another bloody room, another bloody knife. She felt it too, he was sure of it, and when she touched his inner thigh, a confidence passed between them no words could ever express. Drew had thought then that Gail might know something about the awakening that he had experienced at the hands of Mr. Brittany. He'd almost asked her if she too knew the man with the petite shape and leathery voice. It was there in her face; a reflection in those deep, craven eyes she had consigned herself to.

Drew saw that same look now in the eyes of the figure before him.

"I know you. My god, I know you. Drew–" the masked viper spoke. Barely more than a whisper, but the words and their foreboding sentiment carried over the entire room, taking on physical force, obscuring the evening's blossoming eroticism. The figure looped its arms up and around to the back of its head, and in one swift, fluid motion removed its mask and revealed the only face that had ever given Drew any real hope since his fall.

"Drew... what are you... it's not... oh, Drew, not you too."

The sentiment this time carried a slightly provocative echo at the end of it; a premonition or perhaps a prayer for what might come next. Drew's night, however, had ended right there.

He'd not realized he'd fallen to his knees at the center of a crowd of onlookers. Lucidity a hammer, Drew scrambled back up onto his feet and stood with his center of gravity lowered for defensive pouncing. He was an animal, controlled by animal urges and given to an animal's unease at unpredictable anomalies.

Gail took a step forward and reached for him with her left hand. Drew extended his stance on his calves and batted her away; to those around him, he looked like an orangutan at the zoo, disturbed from a deep sleep by a raucous crowd.

"Drew, it's okay. Please, dear–" behind Gail's words the music underwent an uptick; blazing, distorted guitars filtered in around an aboriginal kick drum and nonsensical, ritualistic snippets of vocals. The beat was inside him, augmenting his own inner rhythm, freshly out of whack and the eye of his sudden emotional storm. Gail looked at him with those same empty, terrified eyes he remembered from all those months ago and inside them Drew saw the shame and pain and complete abandonment in her soul and it was all he could take. Without another moment's hesitation, he turned and ran through the crowd that had encircled them, pushing people over and lunging up the stairs out into the puddles of the night. Drew's first step burst a perfectly inverted image of the club's sin-red marquee before he was in his car and speeding away in tears.

"Oh Drew, not you too…"

'Yes. Me too,' Drew thought as he stopped at the first liquor store he could find and bought the largest bottle of alcohol he could afford. Later, sequestered in his apartment, he sought release in cheap scotch and skin mags, trying desperately to blot out the pounding in his temples that announced the end of all things. But the pounding brought the hazy, 8-bit image again, only this time clearer, more discernible. A giant spider with human limbs for legs and a woman's face. It squeezed something inside of him, and the world went black, only returned when the voice on the other end of the receiver spoke.

"Oh but Drew, you found *me*, remember?"

"Where. Just tell me where," Drew begged, teeth gritted and blood in his eyes.

"1422 South Euclid."

Somewhere inside him, Drew had made the first of his final steps.

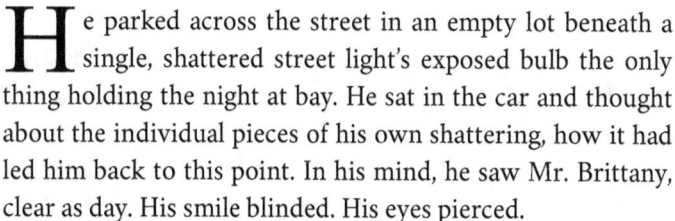

He parked across the street in an empty lot beneath a single, shattered street light's exposed bulb the only thing holding the night at bay. He sat in the car and thought about the individual pieces of his own shattering, how it had led him back to this point. In his mind, he saw Mr. Brittany, clear as day. His smile blinded. His eyes pierced.

This was not a memory. The longer Drew held the image in his mind, the more he became convinced it was a communication. The man was a sorcerer, some high-level black magician who acted as emissary for whatever it was Drew had begun a dialogue with back at the cabin. And if Mr. Brittany had power, perhaps Drew could have it as well. Maybe that was the end result here: power.

"That's insane," he said aloud, but found no reassurance in this proclamation. The facts remained the facts: the escalating visions, the phone calls, and finally, last night.

Drew left his keys in the car when he exited and started for the building across the street.

To Drew, this particular part of the city had always looked like the mandible of a monstrous creature, a lacerating maw of malevolence ready to snap shut and severe whatever was unfortunate enough to be left inside. The buildings stank like rotted teeth, all charred and forgotten, black with age and detritus and blood, real or invisible. The three-flat before him was no different, other than it was the only structure not condemned for as far as the eye could see. Garbage swirled in the wind, stuck to the fences and swung from the rubble that lay scattered across everything, ornaments of disease. Just in front of his destination, another sodium street lamp lapped at the night in frazzled bursts of radiated distress meant to alleviate the darkness.

It failed.

He stood before the door, a large iron-framed industrial portal with a frighteningly simple set of numbers scrawled across its face in red marker.

1422

He knocked, and the transition was complete. The door opened with a strangled creaking to reveal a stairwell. The first subtle strains of a dark and ethereal music reverberated up from what sounded like a great depth. A black shape stood just beyond the threshold; he could feel it contemplating him. Drew's eyes squinted, pulled him forward even as his feet involuntarily took a step back. He could make out the curved lines of a cloak and hood. The figure disappeared into the shadows for an instant and then stepped forward just as the street light flickered on again for the briefest of moments. It was only a glimpse, but in that glimpse Drew caught a trace of distinctly feminine features. Supple chin, angular cheekbones and… breasts, naked in the night. Tall leathery boots stopped at mid-thigh, black meridians that only served to accentuate the pale flesh that emerged from beneath them. He felt himself stiffen, felt the old familiar rush, a junkie reconditioning his reserves. And when she stepped back and beckoned him inside, Drew followed without a thought for the consequences.

～

He had begun to sweat. He thought of the hopeless, forlorn look on Gail's face upon her reveal at the club, the epiphany that her fall from grace had doubled once she'd discovered she was not alone.

The woman led him through a series of filthy corridors, her boots clicking against yellow, corroded concrete, a meter of the distance they would travel to hell. A single exposed bulb cast a yellow hue that made it impossible to see anything for what it really was. The walls were rotted through; girders laid bare, and the musk of exposed pipes choked him, a testament to an ancient industry and the sickness that had consumed it. The music grew louder, more distinct, ultimately revealed as screams of varying intensities and pitches arranged in a mildly melodic pattern. He'd never heard anything like it before, and it made him uneasy. But then he caught another glimpse of thigh through the billowing cloak before him and his appetite commandeered his threat processing faculties.

Eventually, they emerged into a room lit by candles, an empty space occupied by nothing but a small altar at its center. The hooded woman turned to him, and he saw her full face for the first time. Her chin was soft, but the flesh of her cheekbones, nose, and forehead was scaled. No, not scaled but scarred, as if she'd been burned. She smiled as she recognized his assessment, reached forward and cupped him at his base, then turned and swiftly straddled the table, parting her legs and arching her back.

Drew moved in to take what was offered.

The copulation escalated quickly. Unable to resist the allure of her flesh, Drew ran both hands beneath the cloak and up the woman's back. Something rough and scraggly met his touch and, repulsed, he lifted the cloth in a single jerk and cast it aside. Hell came immediately with the subsequent revelation and Drew began to scream.

Where the woman's posterior should have been, directly above where he moved inside her, there was a face. Not a human face, but a face none the less: eyes, nose, mouth. It leered at him, unmistakable in two things: sentience and malevolence. It smiled, its lips more akin to a wound than anything communicative. In his horror Drew saw teeth, terrible teeth that looked like cancerous tissue cut and bloodied inside a kidney or lung. These teeth began to jostle and quake as the thing before him began to laugh. He tried desperately to extract himself, but its inner muscles became vice-like, trapping him inside. Drew stumbled backward to the floor, but the horrible face moved with him, its movements spastic and labored. He remained attached, his legs folding beneath him as his sex pulsated with an infusion of rhythm.

It was milking him.

Great blank swathes of Drew's sanity capsized as the monstrosity reared up before him on what had previously been a woman's arms. Its orientation changed then; the hooded head swiveled down and turned around completely; the laughing, leering face of the abomination came up to look him in the eye, the flesh outlining its features slick with the sweat of their coupling.

It looked like a spider with human limbs as legs.

"Drew," it cooed, the wound a sickening smile, "you must finish inside me. Life cannot be wasted." It was Mr. Brittany's voice but rendered with the same faraway crackle of the music upon his arrival. Arms behind him, Drew scrambled along the floor backward. No use, the thing still moved with him, absolutely refused to let him go. Slathering and exhausted Drew finally collapsed onto his back and watched in abject horror as his captor straddled him and began gyrating faster and faster, driving them both to a stupendous climax.

"Feed me. Give me your lives, so that I may use them as I see fit."

Drew's repulsion drowned beneath the first waves of a massive tide of pleasure; it lapped at the shore of his mind, pulled him under a deluge of ecstasy that unlocked something deep and primordial inside him. In his mind's eye, he stood at the precipice of the known world, the shore of the lake by the cabin, beneath those cold stars once more. Drew's eyes turned inward, stared into the night sky and a massive eye blinked open and filled him with the knowledge that wherever he went from here, he would never be thirsty again.

A COLLECTION OF DESIRES

Mark found April on the top of her apartment building, a half-drank bottle of whiskey in one hand and a loaded forty-five in the other. It was Tuesday.

"Baby, please…"

"Just go away. I don't want you here. I need to think."

April was riding close to the end of her rope and wasn't in the most stable state of mind; if Mark wasn't careful something bad could happen to her. Or him. He approached with caution.

"Where the fuck did you get that?"

"My mom's. Stopped by to see her after work and snatched it out of the hat box she thinks she hides it in."

"How doesn't the facility know your mom has a handgun?"

"What the fuck does it matter, Mark?"

"Take it easy, baby."

"Don't tell me to take it easy! Jesus! I'm sick and fucking tired of people telling me to take it easy," April's words came apart mid-admonishment as sobs reduced her face to a broken mask; for a moment she looked on the verge of collapse.

"You will get through this. I promise. I can help."

"You're not going to help me pay my rent, Mark. I appreciate it, but until we're under the same roof, I'm not about to be your charity case."

They'd talked a lot about moving in together recently; April was ready, but really only because of her rent situation: the lawyer asshole who owned her building had already raised the rent over a hundred dollars in the last six months and now he'd apparently done it again.

"How much?"

"How much? Two hundred fucking dollars, that's how much. Look, Mark, I need to know there's a future in this, that there's a future in you and me."

"April, I want to move in with you, but I've gotta take care of a few things first…"

"This again."

"What again?"

"What? Mark, you keep saying you have things to take care of, but you can never tell me what. How am I supposed to interpret that?"

It was true. Mark had not been able to provide the specifics requested, and it had put a tangible strain on their relationship of late. He wanted to alleviate the situation, he wanted to move in with April, and he was pretty sure she believed him about that, which no doubt made his behavior that much more frustrating to her. Good intentions or not, nothing changed the fact that before he and April could move in together, there were serious issues Mark had to address, chief among them the fact that he was fairly certain he still had part of a human skull adrift somewhere in his living room closet. That, and maybe a box with a severed index finger somewhere in his bedroom.

Maybe.

"Look, April, it's just that I'm…"

April raised the gun and pointed it at Mark.

"So help me god if you say you're fucking someone else I will blow your fucking brains out."

Jesus. She meant it.

"I'm not fucking anyone else. April, I love you." It was the first time he'd said it out loud, and it had the desired effect; Mark watched the anger leave April's body in a tremendous sob. He took his cue, moved in and put his arms around her; the embrace allowed him the leverage to take the gun from her. Once he had it, he guided them back from the ledge, and they took a seat on the small riser they sometimes used as a bench when they came up here to watch the stars. He let April cry for a while, then after enough time had passed, Mark hit her with an idea he'd been toying with ever since the last rent increase.

"What if I talk to him?"

"Who? My landlord?"

"Yeah. Just a friendly little chat? It shouldn't be that hard to find his office online," Mark knew what he wanted to do to Andre Bitterman, Esq.; the same thing he had done to three unknowns in the last two years. His first, the day he graduated with his Masters. Two and three had come six and twelve months later, respectively. Number three had gone bad: a local detective's son. Mark had come close to getting caught on that one, and when he realized he'd gotten away with it because they'd ended up pinning the murder on some idiot drug dealer the kid had been fucking, Mark learned first hand that scandal forces closure real quick. Still, that one had been close enough that he'd built a damn against the urge ever since. But there were cracks in that damn, and he was slipping, of that Mark was certain. Someone was going to have to be sacrificed to this dark god in his blood sooner rather than later, and he'd like nothing better than for it to be April's landlord.

"You'll find him and what? You're not going to intimidate my landlord out of raising my rent Mark; you're just going to end up in jail. Besides, it's not like it's only me. Everyone that lives in my building just got jacked. UH! That cunt deserves a painful fucking death."

"He does. All the better reason to let me talk to him."

April regarded Mark warily.

"What's that supposed to mean?"

Mark breathed deep. It was no mistake he was attracted to her - April tended bar at night, but during the day she went to horror movie make-up school. And she was good too; she had a deep appreciation of the blood and gore most people recoiled from. April drank it deep; Mark had seen her, in theatres and at home, with Savini, Nictero, even Dean Miller. April couldn't turn away, she was too busy studying the gore, comparing it to her own limited experience with the real world, a summer-long stint at an animal hospital when she was eighteen. He'd thought he'd seen the look in her before he'd even mustered the nerve to speak to her. Later, after they'd been dating long enough for her to be safe and him to have learned her tastes in fantasy, Mark couldn't help wondering if those fantasies could be teased out into the real world. However, his curious aspect answered directly to his conscience: what would it do to his own insatiable short-comings if he were to bring another down into this amoral mire with him?

"Might be a lot of fun," Mark said as matter-of-factly as he could manage. Exposing himself like this made him want to laugh. Or cry, he wasn't sure.

"What?"

"I mean... oh, fuck it. What I mean is I long to do some-thing horrible to Bitterman. To cut him, burn him, I don't even know what. You said it yourself; the cunt deserves a painful death. And…" here was the big one, "… before you ask, it wouldn't be the first time."

April's response was a cold, hard stare that told Mark he'd probably just crucified his relationship.

"I'm sorry. I just…" What was he thinking? There was no recovery from this one.

"That stain in your trunk?"

Number three. Yeah, it'd been that bad.

"April look, don't say anything, okay? Just let me walk away. You'll never hear from me again."

Mark lowered his head - a touch dramatic yes, but with good reason - and began to walk toward the stairwell.

"Mark. Mark!" April caught up to him, took his hand in hers. He raised his head and looked into her eyes. Inside he could see her soul, and it was black and crimson and more beautiful than even those he'd taken for himself.

"I always suspected there was something in you. Some innate hostility…" the strains of admiration in April's voice made Mark's heart flutter.

"You're not disgusted?"

"Disgusted? Baby, I'm so turned on I can barely keep my hands off you. Let's go down to my place so you can tell me exactly what it is you want to do to my landlord."

"Us. What I want *us* to do to your landlord."

At that moment her smile had the wattage of a thousand suns, and for the first time in a long time, Mark felt truly happy.

"Y ou'll never believe what Mary told me today."

They were eating at the little Italian place down the street; restaurants were a less-than-frequent treat these days, but it was their seven month anniversary, and April and Mark had never been closer.

"That she's in love with you? I could have told you that."

April smiled and threw a cherry tomato at him.

"No. Dickhead. Look, if you don't want to hear…"

"Sorry. Go ahead, what'd she tell you?"

"Okay, well, so she's been snooping around online for anything about Bitterman, right? And so she ends up finding an ad he posted on Craig's List."

Mark put his fork down. She had his attention.

"What kind of ad?"

April took a sip of beer and smiled, "Listen."

She took another, larger sip while scrolling through her phone. After a moment she stopped.

"Ahem, 'Wealthy older man seeking 18-23-year-old males for mutually beneficial relationship. WEALTHY and looking to share with the right person. MUST BE ATTRACTIVE, OVER 6 FEET TALL AND UNDER 180 POUNDS.'"

"You've got to be fucking kidding me. Let me see that."

April handed Mark the phone.

"How do you know it's Bitterman?"

"See that number right there? Same number on the recent ads for vacancies in the building."

"He can't be that stupid."

"Probably not, but I doubt he handles the apartment stuff himself, assistant probably confused his numbers."

Mark thought for a moment before he continued.

"This is how we get him, April. This is it."

"You gonna answer the ad?"

Mark nodded.

"I knew it! Baby, you are bad ass! But don't let that pig put his butter fingers all over your-"

"No worries there. Look. Remember how I told you that

James and Evelyn asked us to house sit for them at the beginning of next month?"

"Oh my god. It's perfect!"

"Yep. Way up there in the Hollywood Hills, nobody but the coyotes to hear what we do to him ."

"Oh, baby. This is the best anniversary present ever."

"Don't say that yet. You haven't seen what I have for you in the trunk."

"Mark! You didn't?"

"It's just something small, but I had to, and see, it turned out to be fortuitous. After all, you're going to have to break in some skills before next month."

"We're really going to do this?"

"It's what I want, and I always get what I want."

April nearly leaped across the table and kissed him. Life was good.

Before they left the restaurant, Mark had April put both their steak knives in her purse.

~

The idea was simple: Mark would answer Bitterman's ad posing as an interested party. Physically he knew he'd fit the bill: with his penchant for flashy dress and fairly lascivious demeanor, Mark entertained little doubt he could incite Bitterman's interest. And the two had never come face to face; the fat fuck probably didn't even know what April looked like. She was just a name on a check.

Mark located the ad online and spent the rest of the night drafting his response.

~

Eight-thirty, two Wednesday's later: Mark arrived at El Cid on Sunset Boulevard and took a spot at the bar. He'd already scoped the place out: the tone of the restaurant was dark and suggestive; in the main seating area an intriguing musical act that incorporated candlelight, synths and mildly suggestive dancing created an atmosphere of mystery and seduction. Perfect. He'd chosen El Cid because of the venue's predilection for theatrical entertainment; it would cover the ins and outs of the conversation he was about to have with his target; another internet hook-up at the bar, ho-hum. They would fade into the background. He tapped his fingers on the bar but received no response from the bartender, who was too busy talking up two rock sluts in black metal t-shirts. Mark had arrived early hoping for a buzz to take the edge off his excitement, but at this rate, he'd just have to control himself. Two minutes later a black Porsche pulled into the lot and parked between the only two open spots.

"Who else?"

Bitterman entered the building and Mark's pulse jumped. In person, this guy was everything he'd ever wanted in a victim: a far cry from the homeless drifters and junkies Mark had broken into the business of killing with, Andre Bitterman was a greedy, arrogant, mean-spirited pig who was also, perhaps best of all, lonely. And with a bio like that Mark was pretty sure that while a great number of people would notice his absence, not a one of them would care. Some might even celebrate. Late sixties at least and looking every day of it, his quarry's hair had long ago resigned itself to fester as a crescent-shaped moon confined to the edges of his pock-marked head. The suit he wore was new and expensive, but its sophistication was undone by his teeth and fingers nails, all cracked and yellow with age. Add to this the fact that despite the lack of hair on Bitterman's head, there was a veritable field of it running the length of his throat, down past the three open buttons that revealed his chest. The man looked like someone who might turn into a billy goat at midnight. Mark laughed at the thought of anyone ever wanting to have sex with him. It was ridiculous, even with the implication of an indirect salary to sweeten the deal.

The lawyer/slumlord stopped just inside the door and picked Mark out first thing. He approached, eyes pinned uncomfortably to Mark's; the forced intimacy felt something akin to spiritual rape.

"You must be Hans," hearing the name now Mark regretted using it; at the time of his initial response, it had sounded masculine, yet slightly exotic. Now it felt phony. Despite the uncertainty this caused, that dark thing inside Mark welled up and took control. There was a fish on the line and he had a path cleared for it; what's more the idea of killing this one with April really lit his fire. Mark reveled in the fantasy for a moment, directing the energy the anticipation for blood inspired in him toward the being before him. As he did, the air between them became electric.

"I'm sure anyone who drives a car like that can figure out Hans isn't my real name. But yes, I'm the one that messaged you."

Bitterman flashed a leathery smile at the bartender and the kid fell in like an automaton.

"Courvoisier, neat."

Mark waited for the bartender to ask his poison. He did not.

"What is your name then, my boy?"

"I'm afraid that's not how this works."

"I beg your pardon. By all means, please tell me, how does this work?"

"You buy me a drink, we take a table and talk for a while. If I like you, we'll take it from there."

Bitterman thought for a moment. His eyes made a show of taking Mark in from head to toe and back. This was a man used to getting what he wanted. Mark understood.

The bartender reappeared with the cognac.

"And a drink for my friend."

"Corona."

They moved to a table.

Mark had been friends with Evelyn since college. They'd tried dating but could never seem to get along when bodily fluids were involved, so they resolved to an intimate friendship: friends with occasional benefits. This ended when Mark met April. Shortly after that Evelyn met James, an actor who'd been lucky enough to land a pivotal role on a new cable drama that took off, and from there everything snapped into place. The four double dated often and everyone enjoyed everyone else's company. Several months later when James and Evelyn eloped, they asked Mark to watch their home, a freshly purchased mansion set back in the enigmatic Hollywood Hills. It was here that Mark lured Andre Bitterman from the restaurant.

When he'd initially contacted Bitterman, Mark had done so through a generic email at work; the company used the account as an administrative contact for shipping issues and as such everyone in the office had access to it, however, Mark was the only person who actively maintained it. During that first exchange, he'd made it clear to Bitterman that he preferred to talk by phone and acquired a 'burner' for just that purpose. From there communication was minimal enough to control tightly: Bitterman was a busy man and

neither he nor Mark's invented Hans were looking for a relationship of the mind. They spoke only one time after the
initial contact and that was to set up their first meet.

First and last.

"Hans, you are full of surprises my boy," Bitterman said as
he walked in through the front door of the house, a post-
modern foyer with hard lines, neon recessed lighting, and an
all-glass armoire that took up the better part of one wall. The
older man checked himself in the mirror and came away
inspired; at what Mark could only guess. They moved into
the kitchen, a large, open room bordered by windows on
three sides. Outside, the moon drifted into place over the
trees that shepherded the backyard's slow descent into the
canyons that ran through the hills here, the strange nether-
world on the outskirts of Hollywood.

"Wine, or perhaps something stronger?"

"Wine. I'm an old man Hans; if I drink too much, my
virility suffers. You wouldn't want me to be unable to
impress you now, would you?"

"I doubt that would be possible," Mark answered through
politely gritted teeth. The Pig had already pawed him several
times since entering, and it was with great excitement Mark
looked forward to what was just around the corner.

Bitterman gave a cold, lecherous smile and accepted the
glass of Cabernet with vigor. He did not, however, sip until
Mark did. Mark had anticipated this, the baseline paranoia
that would accompany an older man of such wealth and
dangerous appetites, so in spite of his dislike for red wine he
poured himself half a glass and downed it in three easy
gulps. Mark shook a little as the tannin ran away with his
tongue, but after a moment the flood of warmth that
emanated up from his stomach smoothed away the edges. He
set the glass in the sink and took a bottle of tequila from the
shelf above. With a sturdy new composure, he poured a

snifter and with the first taste felt himself relax into the situation.

"You're my first."

This was improv; Mark wasn't quite sure where it had come from, but the idea of a little role play appealed to him.

"Really?"

Mark-as-Hans nodded.

"But I am eager. Imagine a dam that's been kept for thirty-five years, imagine the force with which it must break."

Bitterman grew visibly excited: beads of sweat appeared on his brow and his hands began to rub the top of the counter in great, circular patterns.

"I can only imagine. And yet, imagination only goes so far. What do you say we dispense with this talking and get to disassembling that damn, brick by brick."

Watching him talk, Mark noted something strange set in around the corners of the older man's eyes: the dark, leathery skin began to swell, forcing his oblong sockets into slits of intense focus. Staring into those eyes, Mark thought he saw the pupils expand as well, a thin crescent of crimson fanning out and around the irises.

The next thing he knew Bitterman was on top of him.

Mark screamed; the man moved quicker than his eyes could track and panic overtook him. Mark pushed at his attacker, but something had happened to his arms; they contained no strength, no will with which to interrupt Bitterman's violent advances.

"Hold on, just…"

"You're not some fucking tease now, are you Hans? Because that would be very bad for you," Bitterman's voice had changed: he no longer sounded like a fat, rich lawyer. He sounded like a monster, all raw and baritone.

"April!"

"If you must call me by your last little girl lover, that is fine. I will take her memory from you in slow, exhausting thrusts."

Andre had both hands on Mark's shoulders, used them to force him to the floor. Mark's mind recoiled further when he felt something thick and fibrous graze the back of his neck in slow circular patterns. What appendage was this?

"Fucking now, April!"

There was a sharp crash and his attacker fell away. Deep red rivulets dappled across Mark's forehead, lips and chin as he turned to see Bitterman unconscious, April standing over him with a meat tenderizing mallet in her left hand, a bloody clump of hair stuck to its studded face.

"Sorry, I had a moment of doubt. I'm over it now."

"Quick, help me get him into the bathroom like we planned. Something isn't right here."

"You mean other than the fact that we just lured a wealthy lawyer into our friends' home to torture and murder him?"

"Yeah. Other than that. Come on; you get the ankles, I'll get the wrists."

The layout of the house was an exaggerated example of the open-space worshipping Mid-Century Modern style, with the kitchen, living room and bedrooms all encased in windows. Add to this a long, Kubrickian corridor, also primarily glass, which connected the sleeping quarters from the social spaces, and what you had was two distinct buildings so isolated from one another that Mark had, on several occasions, attended a party in one that was undetectable in the other. Two smaller bedrooms flanked the corridor about halfway towards the kitchen from the Master, so those were fairly isolated as well. James and Evelyn planned to populate these rooms with a family; would the ghost of this night remain to terrorize their childrens' sleep? Mark had not thought of this until now, but necessity murdered any regret he might have momentarily experienced.

It was to the Master Bedroom Mark and April carried her landlord. At the back of the room was a full-size bath, inside of which they had made their preparations. A marble countertop ran the length of the room, a deep-basined sink in the center, a walk-in shower at the far end.

The shower was a marvel of eclectic modern design: enormous slabs of slate for walls, these rose on a stone dais to connect to a dropped ceiling that imitated the smooth contours of the transition from the floor. Instead of a glass door, there was a riveted steel one, equally snug at top and bottom. It was the 're-appropriated industrial" look, James had explained to Mark. For a guy whose fame and fortune had come unexpectedly, James retained a wry, sardonic approach to everything in his life, especially his money; it was one of the things that made Mark like him so much.

"Our bathroom cost more than some people's homes," he quipped when they'd shown it to Mark the first time. Mark was happy for Evelyn and equally happy for James. They were good people in a world Mark felt sorely lacked the type, and while the question could be raised why, if he liked them so much, he felt comfortable murdering a man in their home, Mark felt this was beside the point. He did what he must to appease the monster in his blood; it was nothing personal.

They deposited the Lawyer's unconscious bulk inside the shower and sealed the door with a padlock. The fact that the door's design made this possible made Mark wonder about its manufacturer's motivations.

"Okay, you have the playlist cued?" Mark asked, fiddling with the laptop he'd previously staged on the counter.

"I do." April handed him her iPod and Mark jacked it in. A

moment later iTunes launched and the name of the playlist lit up the top of the screen.

"Wonder Torture Garden?" Mark laughed.

"Well, Wonder Torture Bathroom didn't have quite the same feel."

April joined in his laughter. Mark hit play and sampled the first ten seconds on his headphones while unfolding a small leather satchel, inside of which were several perfectly kept medical instruments. A USB ran from the left side of the computer to a small grey box several inches to its right. He clicked a button on this, and a moment later a short series of tones went off inside the shower, muffled by the stone walls and steel door but audible enough to confirm success.

"Now what?"

"Now we wait."

"Feels weird."

"Yeah, first one does."

"Tell me about yours," April drew closer, put her stomach against his, slid her hands into Mark's pockets.

"Surprisingly, I don't actually remember it that well. Just the feeling of fiercely wanting to get through it. A very clipped experience, probably nerves."

"Makes sense, I guess."

Mark pushed another button and speakers placed throughout the room crackled to life, a low-level white noise filling out their presence.

"How do you feel?" He asked as they made their way back out to the kitchen.

"Exhilarated, I guess."

"You guess?"

"I feel strong, you know? Like, kind of unstoppable."

"It didn't seem that way when I had to call you out to do your part."

"I'm good now. Trust me."

"I do, I just can't have you hesitating when it counts."

"I'm good."

"Cool."

Mark poured two tequilas this time and they took their drinks back to the bathroom. Outside, the lights from the pool that wrapped around the house like a horseshoe cast moving patterns across the glass, phantoms to guide them on their dark journey.

A disembodied moaning now filled the bathroom by way of the speakers. The sound gave the room an atmosphere of misery.

"Sounds like our boy is waking up. Now comes the fun part."

Mark moved to the computer and punched the volume key several times with his index finger. Inside the shower, a new sound began to echo off the stone and steel, its reverberations muffled but chilling: the sounds of pigs being slaughtered.

"Jesus. Even through the fucking stone that's terrifying," Mark said.

"It should be, I had Brad at the sound lab pull everything he could find on death. There's layers of pigs being slaughtered run over with kids screaming at their mother's funeral, a couple car accidents. There's even what's supposed to be the audio from a scene in an actual snuff film, a guy in a mask hacking another guy to pieces with a machete."

"Jesus Christ, you are one sick fuck."

April grabbed Mark's junk through his tight hipster jeans and kissed him deeply.

"But I'm a good fuck, right?"

"Goddamn right."

Mark kissed her hard on the mouth and before he realized it, he had April on the floor, taking her from behind, her fists braced against the shower door.

"I want to listen to that bastard cry while you fuck me," she said, and began to pound on the door with her palm between Mark's thrusts.

"You hear me, fuckhole? After Hans here gets done fucking me the way you thought you were going to fuck him, we're going to kill you. Slowly!"

April's taunts to Bitterman drove Mark into a frenzy, and he began to pump into her harder. April started to shriek in exaggerated passion, and the sound of their increasingly hysterical copulation, in turn, provoked escalating responses from Bitterman, who began to plead with them between sobs, his voice brought out to them via a well-placed microphone and another set of speakers.

"Please. Please!!!" the cries drove April into a fierce orgasm, Mark right behind her. Then, right in the middle of her ecstasy, April's cries of passion stopped dead, as did the grinding rhythm of her hips. Mark was left gasping, inches shy of his own finish line.

"What... what the hell are you doing? Don't stop; I'm right there!"

But Mark's passion ebbed as well when he realized there was a new sound in the room: Laughter; it permeated everything.

"What the fuck?" Mark said, the chill in his spine chasing away the fire in his groin.

"Is he laughing?" Just as April asked the question, something hit the inside of the shower door hard enough to startle them both to their feet.

"Jesus, what the hell?" This time a volley of blows exploded against the door and they watched in terror as the thick metal rivets began to pop, the steel ballooning outward. When the assault ceased, they saw parts of the metal had peeled away like the petals on a flower, revealing a small hole that looked in on their makeshift prison.

"Mark... you should have never chosen me for your little games. I came for your ass, but I'll be leaving wearing your blood. All of it."

Mark's spine was on fire now, pure, unadulterated terror coursing through every inch of his body. He turned to April and saw she was no different. What the hell had they come across? Whatever it was, it was still talking, its voice no longer Bitterman's at all. It sounded like something he recognized; recognized but couldn't quite put a finger on.

"I am a collection of desires dear boy, and I always get what I wa-"

Mark turned and spiked the volume on the iPod, instantly drowning the voice in the sound of slaughtered pigs and children screaming. Another blow opened the hole into the shower even wider and for just a brief second and in spite of his attempts to look away, Mark saw something through that hole; a deep red eye and a row of silver teeth caked with thick, black liquid that sluiced from between them. A thousand horror movies took a bite out of reality and Mark felt something inside him snap. It was the same something that had narrowly saved him as he fled the scene of number three, the detective's son's body left in the park he'd first seen him in. That same instinct sounded off, and Mark's intuition took over; he had April by the wrist and led her through the house, back up through the corridor that joined the bedrooms to the main floor plan.

"Where's the car?" his words were frantic, a series of insistent alarms throttling him from the inside, the certainty their death lay mere moments up the clock from here.

"On the street, where you told me!"

"Shit!" even before the explosion sounded behind them, Mark knew they'd never make it to the street. They hit the kitchen just as what sounded like a very large animal with sharp claws scrabbled across the roof, dopplering from behind them out to their left. A second later, out of the corner of his eye, Mark saw a large, black shape leap from the roof into the yard. He quickened his pace and cut a sharp one-eighty just as the Thing threw itself through the window thirty feet to their left. Glass was everywhere, and a terrible howl filled his ears, almost drove him to his knees. Mark was shocked to realize it was April, screaming bloody murder behind him.

They made it back into the corridor they had emerged from only moments before just as their pursuer hit the kitchen - Mark could hear its talons tearing the stone floor to shreds as it gained on them. A second later there was a tug on his arm and before he could even register the loss, April was torn from his grip; the momentum sent Mark spilling backward onto his side, a jolt of pain sending tears to his eyes and snot pouring from his nose.

"Maaaaaarrrrkkkk…" April's scream disappeared into the house behind him. Stunned, Mark sat in silence waiting for their attacker to return for him.

It did not.

~

Three months later.

Mark finished his shift at the bar and carefully evaded the attention of the girl in the corner booth. He'd left with her the night before, would not do so again. Never the same girl two nights in a row; he'd learned this the hard way, soon after relocating to New Orleans, after learning the truth about himself.

"I am a collection of desires. I always get what I want." This is what the Bitter Monster - as Mark had come to call the thing that had assaulted him that night in James and Evelyn's - said just before taking April from him. At the time,

Mark could not understand why it had not killed him as well. Three days later and halfway to his new home in New Orleans he'd figured it out. It only took one good, long look in the mirror to see the tiny slivers of crimson filling in around his irises, to understand that the Bitter Monster hadn't chosen him, Mark had chosen it. Set on a path of destruction from the time he took his first life, Mark had been on a collision course with the evil that lurked in the hearts of only the vilest of human beings, what he had referred to during his introspective monologues as 'the dark thing inside his blood.' Only, it had found him first. Mark knew he could continue to fuck as many of the barflies as he wanted, but the moment he tried to make any real connection, he would be back on the path to taking another life. And as much as his hands longed to play in the blood of another, the same desire also prevented him from ever being anything other than alone.

www.ingramcontent.com/pod-product-compliance
Lightning Source LLC
Chambersburg PA
CBHW071127100726
47908CB00008B/2512